(Isabelle Randall) I. R.

A lLady's Ranche Life in Montana

(Isabelle Randall) I. R.

A lLady's Ranche Life in Montana

ISBN/EAN: 9783337119331

Printed in Europe, USA, Canada, Australia, Japan

Cover: Foto ©Andreas Hilbeck / pixelio.de

More available books at **www.hansebooks.com**

A Lady's Ranche Life

in Montana.

BY

I. R.

LONDON:

W. H. ALLEN & CO., 13, WATERLOO PLACE,

PALL MALL, S.W.

1887.

LONDON:

PRINTED BY W. H. ALLEN AND CO., 13 WATERLOO PLACE

PREFACE.

THIS is an age of Emigration. We are sending out our sons, and brothers, our cousins, our friends, and even our daughters and sisters, to all parts of the world; or, if we are not yet sending them we are debating whether we shall send them, and so we begin to feel the want of a kind of emigration catechism; but it is easier to draw up the questions for such a catechism than to find the proper answers; questions enough there are which we are ready to ask of those who have gone out. "What sort of country is it that you have gone to? Is it cold or hot—beautiful, or bare—healthy or unhealthy? How do you live there ? What do you do ? What do you get to eat ? How do you spend your time ? Can you get servants, or must you do all the work yourself ? Can you earn a living ? Must you have capital to start with, or can you work your way up to a livelihood without an allowance from home ? What sort of people do you live with ? are they all cowboys, or ruffians, or desperadoes; or are there any neighbours that you would care to have as companions, or even to welcome as friends ? Is the life a very hard one ? Do you really enjoy it, or do you heartily wish yourselves at home again ?" There are other still more important questions to be asked: "Does the Church do her duty to her children in those far-off lands, and minister to them, and provide them with all those helps to a good and holy life, never more needed than where men are struggling for the very means of existence, and never more welcomed than by many an emigrant ? " We wish we could say the Church at home has at all risen to the feeling that it is indeed one of her highest duties to provide for the spiritual needs of the thousands that leave our shores for foreign lands. Certainly no nobler work could be found for the brave young hearts and eager spirits of those who leave our English homes, than the ministering to the bands of settlers, and anyone who undertook that work would find more than enough to cheer him in brightening, strengthening, encouraging, purifying, and ennobling the hearts and characters of our emigrants. If little trace of an answer to this supreme question, "What does the Church do for you?" can be found in the pages of this little book, it is because no satisfactory answer can be given. To the other questions, and to many more besides, answers will be found in the Letters which the book contains. The Letters were written to friends at home by a young bride who went out with her husband immediately after her marriage. They are a faithful and unvarnished Record of a Settler's Life. We find in them a description of the daily record of work. There were hardships to bear, and struggles to be made. What we should chiefly gather from the

Letters is that the firmness, and determination, and courage which go to form the English character will carry even those who come from the comforts of an English home well through the hardships and the struggles. The life pictured in these pages was certainly not a gloomy one. There is in it abundance of the charm of beauty of country, of genial companionship, of interesting novelty of surroundings, of the excitement of adventure, of the keen sense of enjoyment that comes from finding that you are able to do for yourself what others used to do for you. There is much to amuse, and not a little to le from this lady's letters. Even masters of our public schools may take a warning not to discourage the study of Greek, when they see how a well-worn quotation from Homer saved one of the Settlers from being hung. The mothers of our young girls may be persuaded that there are many more useless, and even harmful, studies for their daughters to engage in than the ignoble art of cooking. Our young ladies may be persuaded that the way to secure woman's rights does not lie in making themselves in dress, manner, and conversation as much like men as possible, but much more in being as much like true women as possible, in all the quickness and readiness of a woman to fit herself to new surroundings, and in all the charm of liveliness, and cheerfulness, and usefulness that makes a man's home bright. Fathers and sons alike will see how clearly these pages show that the idle, and weak, and useless, if they do little good and much harm at home, are likely to do less good, and more harm, in other countries. Above all, those who find it hard in overcrowded land to get an opening for work, may see that it can be found in other countries. There are many who find a town life dreary, and who dread its luxury and its temptations, who shrink from the office stool, and doubt whether their honesty will stand firm in the transactions ot business—many who love the open life of the country—for whom mountain and wood, field and flora, clear skies and wide plains, even storm and frost, have an attraction—many who love to have for their companions the hardy and the

bold, the more unsophisticated and uncon-
ventional—who long to carve out their own
fortunes, even though they have something tough
to carve—these, and many others, may find that
there is room for all this in a Settler's life, and
better still, they will find that there is room for
honest industry, and brotherly fellowship, and
the softening influences of gentleness and kind-
ness, for self-denial, for the give and take of a
Settler's home, for the courtesy and hospitality that
fit the new country as well as the old—in short,
that there is plenty of room for true manhood,
upright, bold, brave, enduring, and self-restrained,
and for true womanhood, tender, true, bright,
gentle, and self-sacrificing, to do its work. We
venture to think that none of them will turn
away disappointed from " A Lady's Ranche Life
in Montana."

A Lady's
Ranche Life in Montana.

———◆———

WHAT quarter of the globe have not Englishmen, and even ladies, not only visited, but lived
in? So, I must confess, I was hardly prepared
for the blank astonishment of all my friends,
when I announced my intention of settling on
the slopes of the Rocky Mountains. After. the
first burst of astonishment, the natural question
was " Where? " But on my replying " Montana," I found, in most cases, I might just as well
have said the Moon, for all the information the
name conveyed.

It really was a hopeless task to explain its whereabouts, when the only places known in America seem to be New York, Chicago, and the Rocky Mountains. "But, my dear," one friend after another would say, "are you really going to a place so outlandish that we have not even heard of it? Are there any white men there (for, of course, there can't be any women), or are there nothing but Indians and grisly bears? Have the natives houses, or do they live in tents and caves, and wear skins? You can't really mean to go there, it's too dreadful. Poor dear, you will most assuredly be murdered, carried off by Indians, or devoured by wild beasts!" Very encouraging, I thought to myself, but replied, cheerfully, that I knew very little about it, but would write and tell them when I got there, if I could get an Indian or a grisly bear to act as postman.

I need not tell you that I did start in spite of it, for here I am, and, as it seems letters *do* leave this barbarous region, I am going to tell you all about it. Of course we crossed the

Atlantic in safety, and of course the captain told someone, who told someone else, who told me, that it was the worst passage on record. I only know it *was* very rough, and I was *very* glad when, after twelve days, we reached New York. Wonderful city, with its Equality and Fraternity, fearful streets, elevated railways and gigantic hotels.

Even on the wharf I found myself regarded by the Custom House officials with a kind of wondering pity. They seemed to think it their duty to find out all about me, and enlivened their disagreeable task by a brisk conversation. "Going to Montana, I see,"—looking at the labels. "Going on a trip? Going to live there, perhaps? Well, I do say." And at last, when the luggage had been turned upside down, the examining official bade me farewell and wished me good luck in my new home, as though I were going on a forlorn hope to the North Pole.

Leaving New York, we made the usual tour to the wonders of Niagara, and so on to

1 *

Chicago. Of course we were assailed by the usual army of railway fiends—book, fruit, and pea-nut sellers; one of the former saying, " Well, if you don't want to buy any books, just *read* this; it's awful good." Chicago I found to be, as they say in the West, "quite a place." Plenty of white men here, at any rate; and such beautiful shops with quite the latest Paris fashions. An old friend of Jem's drove us round the boulevards and parks in the neatest of stanhopes, with a pair of horses which I fell quite in love with. And oh! the new racing club—an infant Sandown. Such a charming place, with its great cool verandah and *such* a lovely ball-room. It made me quite loth to leave the city of cattle, cable-cars, and tinned meat manufacturers, *en route* for St. Paul.

There surely, I thought, there will be Indians and mud huts, gamblers and miners in picturesque costumes, desperadoes with silver-mounted revolvers and bowie-knives; in short, all the accessories of the frontier. Nothing of the kind; only Chicago on a smaller scale. Yet

many people must recollect St. Paul as I had
imagined it, and that not so very many years
ago. But as we took our places on the Northern
Pacific Pulman car, booked for the Far West,
thick and fast came visions of buffalo and grisly
bear, and many a stirring encounter with that
" terror of the West " ; in imagination I could
hear the wild yell as Crow and Piegan, Snake
and Blackfoot, met in furious onslaught, and
scalped one another with relentless ferocity.

" Tickets, please." Oh ! what a shattering of the
illusion! Can I really be going to the Far West ?
Can it really be as wild as my friends pictured it,
when the journey is so easily accomplished, and
travelling brought to such a pitch of perfection,
as regards comfort, as it is on these Pulman
cars.

At Dickinson I really did think I was getting
West when the advent of our train was signalled
by a salvo of revolver shots from a knot of men
in broad-brimmed buckskin hats, blue shirts, and
such funny leather leggings, with leather fringes
down each side. Jem informed me these were

cowboys; and very fine, handsome men some of
these "boys" were; but I should have liked
them quite as well if they had left those
horrid "shooting-irons," as they call them, at
home. After a few hours the train reached
Minquesville, where I was further surprised by a
new development of cowboy. The train stopped,
and in swaggered two men, dressed to the
highest pitch of cowboy dandyism, accompanied
by a *lady*, dressed in a dark travelling suit of
the latest fashion, while her companions were
adorned with the usual broad-brimmed white
buckskin hat, blue shirts, embroidered brown
velvet coats, a red handkerchief round their
waists, with silver-mounted revolvers stuck in
them, embroidered buckskin leggings with very
long fringes and, to complete the equipment, a huge
pair of silver Mexican spurs. Here, I thought,
really are a couple of true desperadoes of the
frontier; but I was quite at a loss to account
for the presence of the lady, for such she
evidently was. Had she been travelling in the
wild West, fallen in love with this bold frontiers-

man, and married him?—for I caught a glimpse of a wedding-ring, which I thought looked very bright and new. However, while I was lost in these speculations the conductor shouted " All aboard," and one of my desperadoes, nodding goodnight to his fellow, left the train; nor did he fail to fire a parting salute as we left the station. I pondered over the lady and the cowboy, and at last concluded that they were starting on their wedding tour, and that this was the sequel to some romantic story. But I racked my brains in vain to account for it, till the black porter put up the berths for the night.

In the morning Jem told me he had most exciting intelligence, and proceeded to tell me that he had learnt, in the smoking-room, the story of the cowboy's bride; but alas! it dispelled all my illusions: she had done no more than I had done myself. The two cowboys proved to be French noblemen, formerly in the French Army, who had married two English girls and were now living at their ranche in Southern Montana, enjoying the free, wild life in this glorious exhilarating air, and amassing fortunes from the increase in their flocks and herds. Jem also told me there were several French gentlemen married and settled in this part of the country.

By this time the train was entering the magnificent valley of the Yellowstone, and I was well content to sit and gaze at the wonderful beauty of the scene. The clearness and brightness of the atmosphere gave a vividness to everything that I had never seen elsewhere. The golden yellow of the grass, the bright red of the brush by the river-side, the blue-black of the masses of pine against the snow, last, and perhaps most beautiful of all, the dazzling white of the snow-mountains, rising up peak above peak into the brilliant blue of this Western sky—all this formed a picture not to be excelled for brilliancy of colouring, and I began to think that this was fairyland. Perhaps it is this wonderful brightness of colour, almost as much as the geysers and other marvels of this beautiful region, that has earned for it the name of " Wonderland."

And so we were carried smoothly along the blue waters of the Yellowstone, past incipient "cities" of one "store" and a "saloon," past log-cabins and "corrals," the mean-looking head-quarters of great cattle kings, counting their cattle by the thousand; past bunches of sleek, fat cattle, who lived apparently on air (so scanty did the grass appear to my uneducated eyes), past an occasional herd of startled ante-lope, until we took our last lingering look at this lovely river and struck off across the open prairie for the Great Divide between the valleys of the Gallatin and Yellowstone. After ascending the slopes of the Divide, amidst most lovely scenery, we at last entered the Bozeman tunnel; and I must confess to an uncomfortable feeling at the thought of having the main range of the mighty Rockies over my head. But we emerged safely at the Bozeman end, and, after admiring the pretty little town, with its odd mixture of small wooden villas and imposing brick structures, steamed slowly out into the famous Gallatin Valley— famous at least in Montana and to all who have heard of Montana, and famous to me, for this is to be my home, amongst the mountains, the cattle, the Indians, and the grisly bears.

"Moreland is the next stop," said the conductor; so as we approached our destination we stood on the platform, between the cars, to see what it looked like. A few buildings, but all very nicely built, met the eye, placed in the midst of a level valley, some eight miles long by six wide, surrounded on all sides by mountains— a veritable park. A few small white farm-houses here and there, and beautiful rivers, with their fringes of trees on both sides. " Prettiest town site in Montana, and the choicest tract of land in the best valley in the territory," says Jem enthusiastically. " Jump out, here we are ! "

It was Friday evening when we arrived, after two and a half days' journey from St. Paul, and we were met at the station, or " depôt," as it is called, by Jem's brother Frank, with the buggy. Mrs. F——, the leader of fashion in Moreland, was at the station to welcome us (so there are women here!). Jem and I drove down home over ditches and badger-holes, until we came to a large gate, which is the entrance into our domain. Down a steep hill, like the side of a railway embankment, and here we are at the door. The house is really pretty ; when we have got all the things up, it will be lovely. I will give you a thorough description of it when all is done.

I bought a sofa, small arm-chair, and music-stand at Chicago. Our party consists of our two selves, Jem's brother Frank, his. friend B—— and our domestics ; an old English couple, by name Morris, and their boy Johnny, whom Jem unearthed in the wilds of Battersea. Mrs. M—— is very nice and quiet, and a good cook. We are living on antelope, wild duck, fish, and prairie chicken.

I spent my first morning unpacking my big box. Nothing broken, except one small picture. I have been unpacking ever since I arrived, and have not a quarter done yet. We have breakfast at 7 A.M., luncheon at 1, and so on ; Mrs. M—— cooks, and I lay the table. The boys are so pleased with knives and forks again ! The weather is lovely, except in the mornings, when we have fires all over the house. On Saturday I had a tea-party; Harry, a cousin of Jem's, and Mr. H——, who rode over from his place, twelve miles off.

I think I shall enjoy my life immensely, and only wish you could all be here. On Sunday we all walked to church, which was held in the parlour at the Moreland Hotel. The parson gave us a long sermon, and we had the usual evening service. The hymns were rather ludicrous; one woman started them, and the rest made a noise. Our walk there was exciting, the night being pitch dark, and we had three or four streams to cross. I managed to clear them all. I have not seen any *wild beasts* yet, though I 've seen plenty of cowboys. We are only a mile from the *town* (eight houses and an hôtel); but only think, in this barbarous region, being only a mile from railway station, telegraph, and post-office! It almost reads like the advertisement of an English country house.

October 27th.

I HAVE been busy all this week cleaning and dusting the house. I find there are a good many household things to be got, so we are going to Bozeman (eighteen miles by road, or three-quarters of an hour by train) to get them. The drawing-room and bed-room will be as nice and pretty as can be wished, with curtains, carpets, &c., but the dining-room will have to wait. Jem and I made a towel-horse; it looks grand, but he hasn't time for much of that sort of thing.

One afternoon we drove up to the horse-ranche, and saw a band of fifty or sixty horses corralled. We were just in time to see them all come galloping down from the hills; the men got them in very cleverly. I have ridden three times on a very quiet mare, Truemaid; she is the last Jem broke, just four years old. The saddle I got from Griffiths and MacDougall fits her very well. My *race-horse*, Daisy, came back from her trainer's yesterday. She is a real

beauty, fit to ride in the Park, and very showy.
I hope I shall be able to use her. Another day
we rode up to the horse-ranche and saw Jem and
Frank branding colts. It was most exciting.
They are driven into the corral, a sort of yard,
generally round, with a fence seven feet high,
made of strong poles laid one on top of the other,
between very strong posts. Then the colts are
lassoed by the front feet and thrown. One man
jumps on their heads, to keep them down, while
the other holds their fore-feet off the ground
with a lasso, and a third brands them. It seems
such a shame, branding the poor little things,
and is a great disfigurement afterwards; but, of
course, it is quite unavoidable, as the horses out
here all run together in the hills, like New
Forest or Exmoor ponies.

All the Englishmen out here have been to
call. I have had a visitor every day, and sometimes two. Mrs. M—— is very willing to work,
and we get on very well. I work in the house
all the morning, and am out with Jem or the
boys all the afternoon; we play whist every

evening. The two boys have started on a week's hunt, and hope to bring back no end of game. We breakfast on trout and whitefish, which we catch every morning, and dine off wild duck, teal, and prairie chicken, the latter as good as grouse, only bigger. I am writing by a log fire, which is too warm, as the sun has come out. The weather is perfect, bright sunny days and cold nights. I think that the air here is quite as good as in Derbyshire, only drier. My piano hasn't come yet, so the drawing-room is left undone; but the photographs and pictures are gradually going up, and look well on the red paper. There was a ball ten or twelve miles from here the other evening; and I heard that the dancing was really not bad. You will hear of me going to one soon.

November 2nd.

WE went to Bozeman on Tuesday, started at
10 A.M. and got back at 8.30, the train being
four hours late owing to a mass of rock having
fallen on the line.   Bozeman is a nice little
town of about 3,000 inhabitants; there are
some rather pretty Swiss-looking villas, which
are the residences of the principal business men.
The main street, which is generally six inches
deep in either dust, mud, or snow, has some good
brick and stone buildings, and boasts of two
villainous hotels, but in the stores (*Anglice*, shops)
you can get any conceivable thing you want, except, perhaps, a Paris bonnet or the last number
of the *Queen*.   We did our shopping satisfac-
torily.   Could anything be nicer than to start
after breakfast, get through all our shopping,
and be back again by 5 o'clock?   I felt exactly
as if we had been up to London and back for the
day.

We are having a very pleasant week all to

ourselves, as the boys are away. One day Jem and I started at 10 A.M., after my work was done, to hunt for cattle. I rode Daisy; she is perfect. Jem has given her to me as a wedding present; and no one else is ever to ride her. She is very showy, and " high lifed," nearly thoroughbred, or " gently raised," as they call it. Some day I may get to riding " bronchos," *i.e.* native horses, which run wild in the hills till they are old enough to break. We did not find the cattle, but had a lovely ride of twenty miles. We had coffee, bread and butter, and buffalo-berry jelly (which is as good as red currant), at a small ranche, and all sat down together with the men. The women waited on us; they were very polite to me, but seemed to look on me as a kind of wild animal. We got back in time for 5 o'clock tea. Mrs. M—— is not strong, but gets on very well. I do all the housemaiding and parlourmaiding.

November 10th.

I REALLY must tell you about our lady callers, for you will have found out by this time that the grisly bears and the Indians are all a myth, that we are living quite a humdrum existence in the midst of the highest civilization, and that life in the Far West at the present day is by no means a succession of stirring adventures by flood and field. My first caller was the lady (they are all *ladies* out here) who supplies us with butter. She came down about 11 o'clock one morning with some butter, and I received her in the kitchen, where we conversed amicably until she took her departure. This, as we afterwards learnt, gave dire offence. It was a *bonâ fide* morning call, and I ought to have received her ladyship in the " parlour " with my best company manners.

Our next callers arrived one afternoon in a buggy; I basely fled, and left Jem to do the honours. As he had not much cultivated the

acquaintance of the softre sex out here, he hadn't
the least idea who they were.   However, he
asked them to come in and sit down, which they
did side by side on two chairs, with their backs
against the wall; they were got up, as he said,
"quite regardless" in feathers and war-paint
—literally the latter.   Imagine a countenance, to
which the sun of Montana had already been
kind, plentifully smeared with rouge and pearl-
powder.   I find this is a common practice out
here, learned, I suppose, from the Indians.   On
leaving they left *cards* for me in the most ortho-
dox style, and we discovered that they repre-
sented the *crême de la crême* of the society of
the neighbourhood.

Jem says he is afraid I shall not find any of
my own sex very congenial companions—in fact,
very much the reverse—but in time, perhaps, the
country may get more thickly settled with
English people, or a better class of Americans
from the older States.

We have made some feeble attempts to get up
lawn tennis and cricket among the English, but

so far without much success. As they say, "A
man doesn't want to hunt for exercise in this
country, where he is hard at work from morn till
dewy eve." It seems ludicrous to look back on
English life, and the oft-recurring question
"What shall we do to-day?" when here it is not
a question of "*What* shall we do?" but "How
in the world shall we find time to do it all?"

Two afternoons we spent in buffalo-berrying and
shooting combined. The novel way of picking
this fruit is to cut down huge branches from the
bushes, and then beat them with a stick; the
berries shower down into a sheet, spread out on
the ground. In this way we soon gather all we
want. Every now and then prairie chicken or
grouse make their appearance upon the scene, or
a duck goes down upon the pool close by, and a
rush is made for the gun; so that the entertain-
ment is of a varied nature.

My drawing-room is lovely. I have put up the
four red curtains on each side of the two side
windows, and the looking-glass between, photo-
graph frames and writing-table underneath. The

other outside wall has one window with red
curtains. I will finish the description when my
piano comes, as the room is not a quarter done
yet. Now for the wild beasts! just in from a
walk and I saw a white weasel, a chip monk, a
pretty little beast with black and white stripes
down its back (something between a squirrel and
a rat), and a white-tailed deer.

November 23rd.

LAST week Jem and I started at 8 o'clock to
ride to Three Forks (a ranche belonging to some
English friends), to buy horses for the Eastern
market. It was a ride of about 12 miles. When
we were half-way there, we met one of the
owners of the ranche coming to see us; he
stopped and made us promise to stay the night,

while he went on to our place to fetch our things. Three Forks is a nice place, and the house very comfortably furnished. As it was being cleaned, we were quartered at the hotel close by. After supper we came into the "parlour" and found half the population, working men and all, assembled to inspect the "stranger." The only female in the room immediately undertook to introduce me all round, which appears to be the custom out here; the ceremony being effected by a general hand-shaking with the accompanying expression, "Glad to make your acquaintance, Ma'am."

We rode home next morning through the foot-hills. The ground was, of course, frozen as hard as a brick, so it was not very good "going." It never is out here, for that matter, as the ground is either as hard as a rock from frost or drought, or else covered with snow, or sticky as glue from wet. The hills were all covered with dry tufts of yellow-looking grass; most unappetizing fodder, I should think; but stock live and thrive on it all the winter, pawing and rooting through the light

snow. Jem says it is cured by the sun as it
stands, in July, and is really like the very best
hay, preserved with all the juices in it.

When we got back, we found the boys had
come home from their hunt, with a waggon-load
of sage hens and small game, but alas! no elk or
deer to show for their pains.

We are beginning the real cold weather now.
Everything freezes in the house at night. The
bread is like a cannon ball, meat and everything
else in the same condition, and the milk a block
of ice. In our bed-room, though we had a fire in
the room over night, we found the water in the
bath frozen solid to the bottom. I rode in the
middle of the day and did not feel the cold in the
least; though Jem's beard and moustache were
a mass of ice, and icicles hung from our horses'
noses, while their bodies were covered with frost.
I suppose one does not feel the cold because the
air is so dry at this altitude, 3,000 feet above the
level of the sea; also because there is no wind,
and the sun is always bright. Yesterday the
thermometer was 12 deg. below zero at noon, and

yet I didn't think it was nearly so cold as it is when we have 10 degs. of frost at home. This "storm," as they call the spell of cold weather, lasted about 10 days; the thermometer at night going down to 30 below zero.

To-day the "Chinook" wind is blowing, the roofs are dripping, the birds twittering and splashing in the puddles, horses galloping about, squealing and kicking up their heels; we have got all the windows open, and it is like spring. This Chinook wind is the warm current of air, which comes roaring, salt laden from the Pacific, melting the snow and changing the depth of winter into spring in a few hours. It is the stockman's best friend, and enables his stock to withstand the rigours of winter without shelter and with no food, except what nature provides in the shape of the dried grasses in the hills.

The thaw brought us three visitors, Englishmen, who rode over to lunch. Of course we were very glad to see them, and it felt very homelike. However, we were suddenly reminded of where we were, by hearing the harsh notes of

wild geese flying over the house, and made a rt
for the rifles ; a volley resulting in the death or
one goose, which came down with a tremendous
thud.   A great big brown Canada goose, weigh-
ing nearly 20 lbs.

December 2nd.

SINCE the thaw, I have been almost living in
the saddle, riding about with Jem, hunting for
two very valuable well-bred mares, which have
disappeared.   I have been over and through the
most awful places ; quaking bogs, wide rivers,
very rapid and almost deep enough to swim a
horse, and through brush which nearly drags one
off one's horse.   The marvel is that I'm alive to
tell the tale.   The worst of it is, we have not
found the mares ; and on arriving home, there was

eport that two noted horse-thieves had been found, camping in the brush, about a mile from here, and that the man, who saw them, had pulled his six-shooter on them, but that they had disappeared in the brush. If they have taken our mares and any others have gone from near here, I suppose a posse of men will pursue them and there will be a fight, and the attendance of "Judge Lynch" will be requested.

They are very much "down" on horse-thieves. Of course I am very sorry for the poor men, but horse-stealing seems to be on the increase and must be put down. It is so easy for the thieves to get away with their plunder in this country. Jem says, last year a posse of men, well armed, pursued a gang of horse-thieves, and, after a pitched battle, were beaten off, and the thieves remained masters of the field. Perhaps it is not so civilized out here after all.

To return to peaceful subjects. You will wonder, perhaps, what we burn out here. There are any amount of cotton-wood trees on our ranche, and the other day we had the steam saw down here, and sawed up enough to last the whole winter. We have such glorious fires, with great logs three and a half feet long, and as big round as a man's body, piled half-way up the chimneys. There are only two rooms with big fire-places, the drawing-room and Jem's den. All the other rooms are heated with stoves, and it almost keeps one man busy, sawing and splitting billets of wood for them.

While they were all busy with the steam saw, I got on Daisy and rode round to see that all the young stock and "bonny brood-mares" were safe. We keep all our best horses close to the ranche for fear of horse-thieves, and I must confess I was in terror, all the time I was out, of meeting some of these gentry, after the report we had heard. Instead of gates out here, they generally have bars, which you have to let down; and as I could not get off, I amused myself with letting down the top bar and jumping the balance, like the "heave gates" in Sussex. Daisy jumped very well indeed. I should like to ride her out hunting at home. All the horses

were safe; my ride was most enjoyable, and I
hope, after a time, to become an accomplished
stock-woman.

In the evening as we sat round the fire—the
boys smoking their pipes—Frank alluded to the
loss of the two mares, which have never yet been
found. I fear they never will be. He said he
thought it was a mistake to keep good stock
under fence, as these horse-thieves know exactly
where to find them. He told a story of an
expert horse-thief who came to a man who had
an extra good lot of horses out in the hills,
and warned him, in a confidential way, that
there were horse-thieves about, adding, "If I
were you, I should bring all my horses in and
keep them in a corral at night." The unsus-
pecting owner acted on this advice. The next
night the horse-thieves came, let down the bars,
and drove off the whole lot, no doubt feeling
much obliged to the owner for gathering the
band for them.

December 5th.

I HAVE been experimenting in cooking lately, as there is no knowing what may happen in a country where servants are so few and far between, and so very independent. I made a lot of those Rock Cakes which I learnt to make at South Kensington. The boys gobbled them up in no time. My next venture was pancakes; and the crowning success, ox-foot jelly. We got the feet for this from a "beef" which we killed the other day. This is our winter supply of beef. Just fancy, in England, getting a whole bullock at a time! Jem wanted to hang it up on a tree just in front of the drawing-room window, saying, "it would be handy when we wanted a steak"; but on this I had to put my veto. Really one could not have that object always in front of one's eyes, and watch it disappearing during the winter. You see it will freeze now and keep till spring, and be cut up as we want it. Beef brings me to potatoes. Montana produces the best in the world; so floury, and the size astounding; some of them weigh four pounds apiece, and one is enough for four people.

December 9th.

ANOTHER cold spell set in yesterday and the cold is intense. I like it, and find I can stand it much better than the men; while they are frozen, I am comparatively warm.

We have been living, until the last few days, on baking-powder bread, but everyone told us it was unwholesome; so the other day Mrs. M—— went to a neighbour's house to learn how to make yeast. Her first batch of yeast bread was like a lump of lead, and nearly *black*; so I tried *my* hand. My bread *was* white, and comparatively light. Last night I made a lemon pudding for dinner. It came out a most beautiful mould; not a bit heavy. We get plenty of milk and cream from our one cow, but now go without butter as it is so expensive to buy. Game and meat we bake in our American cooking-stove, which does them very well. I always make the puddings in the morning, so as to have them ready by dinner-time.

You ask about our domestics. Mrs. M—— is tolerably cheerful and hard-working. M—— is slow, but always seems to be pottering about doing something; and Johnnie is useful in odd jobs, cleaning knives, boots, &c. On the whole, considering they come from the slums of London, and how little we knew about them, they have turned out better than could have been expected.

Frank and I always wash up after luncheon and dinner, as Mrs. M—— never gets the things as clean as she might do. They always put soap in the water to wash dishes, &c., out here, which was a novelty to me; however, Frank had learned that in his bachelor days, and put me up to it.

December 23rd.

SINCE I last wrote we have had our first heavy snowfall to a depth of from eighteen to twenty inches; it is hard on the stock out of doors, and a great plague to me indoors, as the house gets so dirty; and, to make matters worse, Mrs. M—— has got a bad foot, and is *hors de combat*, and so I have to do everything. Luckily, as it is snowing so hard, the men can't go out much, so they all help me. Frank is a capital cook, and helps me a great deal.

Our Christmas party has had to be put off—a great disappointment, as it is an engagement of a year's standing. Some of the Englishmen from Three Forks were coming, but the storm is so bad that they could not easily get here. The Christmas pudding is achieved — a great triumph, as we all had a hand in it. Frank and I cut up the suet, and we all amused ourselves one evening stoning the raisins; I stirred all the ingredients up in a large tin basin, and it smells quite the proper thing. Frank has just come running in, and flourished a huge piece of beef in my face with great glee. It is the Christmas sirloin which he and Jem have just sawn out of the frozen carcass, which I mentioned to you before.

December 30th.

BEFORE I can begin to write this letter the ink must be put down by the fire to thaw out, as it is frozen solid. I 'm getting quite used to the water freezing in my basin while I 'm washing my hands, and the towels freezing stiff before I can dry them! Christmas-day was lovely. I tried walking in snow up to my knees, but stuck at last in a drift, and had to be ignominiously pulled

3

out by main force. In the evening, if our party was not large, it was very merry. The sirloin was pronounced first-rate, and equal to the very best English beef; the pudding was a great success, light, but no crumbling, and we lit it up in due form. We toasted our absent friends in lager beer, and enjoyed ourselves generally. We had all donned our best bibs and tuckers in honour of the occasion, and at last retired to the drawing-room, where I played the accompaniments to hunting songs, till everyone was hoarse. Then we fell upon Frank to tell his famous hanging story, which he did, after much pressing, to this effect :—

A few years ago, he went in the autumn to Oregon, to buy a large drove of horses to drive to Montana for sale; but on arriving there, he found the prices too high to justify the investment, so the enterprise was abandoned. He knocked about there for some months, and made the acquaintance of certain famous frontier characters, more adventurous than respectable. Amongst others the famous Hank Vaughan, who fought a

desperate duel, in which the combatants clasped
their left hands, and emptied their six shooters.
Both men fell, but, marvellous to relate, both
recovered.

However, to return to Frank's adventures. He
was away from stores and civilization a good
deal: at one time with the Umatilla Indians, and
at another in mining camps in the mountains,
and so gradually his appearance resembled that of
a Western desperado, or "bad man," much more
than an Oxford graduate. In the spring, he
started on horseback for Montana. Unfortunately for him, as it eventually turned out, on the
same day, from the same place, and on a horse of
the same colour, started a well-known desperado,
who had robbed and murdered a man somewhere
close by. The murderer travelled fast—naturally;
so did Frank, for some reason or another, and
both being well mounted, they made about the
same distances each day.

Meanwhile a description of the murderer had
been sent forward, and the Sheriff started,
from some point down the trail, to intercept

3 *

him. Early one morning Sheriff and murderer met.

"Throw up your hands," shouted the Sheriff.

"Read your warrant," was the murderer's cool reply.

As the unfortunate Sheriff lowered his pistol to draw the warrant from his pocket, quick as a flash the murderer shot him dead, and galloped off.

For some days Frank, quite unconscious of the double tragedy that had been enacted, pursued the same route as the murderer. At one place they both exchanged their tired horses for fresh ones. Soon after this they must have taken different routes, and Frank arrived at a noted mining city. Strolling through the town, he was pointed out to the Sheriff as the Oregon murderer. He had sold or lost his revolver, and the empty scabbard hung at his belt. The Sheriff observing this, and knowing the desperate character of the man for whom Frank was mistaken, supposed he had his pistol concealed, and ready for immediate use. Consequently he deemed, I suppose, discretion the better part of valour, and went off in search of the Deputy-Sheriff to make the arrest.

Meanwhile the pseudo murderer mounted his horse, and cantered gaily along on his journey. After riding some miles, he was suddenly aware of a horse galloping rapidly up behind him, and heard a shout:

"Throw up your hands!"

Not being of a nervous disposition, he treated the summons as a joke, and commenced some jocular reply, which was rudely cut short by the ugly sight of a pistol pointed at his head; whereupon he hastily did as he was bid, and threw up his hands. The next second he dropped his right hand, intending to produce his empty scabbard as a proof of being unarmed, which ill-advised movement nearly cost him his life. In fact, after his arrest the Deputy-Sheriff told him that it was little short of a miracle that he did not instantly shoot him, when he dropped his hand, believing him, of course, to be a desperate character, and that he had dropped his hand to seize the pistol, which is usually carried in the scabbard on the belt round the man's waist.

Frank's next move was to ask the Sheriff to read his warrant; which he did, with his eye and pistol on Frank; giving the warrant extempore without running his eye over the document. He had already heard of the fate of the former Sheriff, and did not intend to be caught by the same manœuvre. Frank then quietly gave himself up, at the same time asserting his innocence. The Sheriff then proceeded to handcuff him and turned the horses' heads towards the town.

On the way they stopped at a "cow" camp, where there were several of the boys. These learnt the supposed crime of the prisoner. Without more ado, they decided to constitute themselves judge, jury, and executioner; the insecurity of Western prisons having been so often demonstrated, it is not surprising that men often want to take the law into their own hands in the case of a desperate character. In vain Frank chaffed, stormed, and expostulated in turn; at last he said, if they would question him, they would find he was not, and could not possibly be the man they took him for. They seemed to be struck with the idea that it would be rather good fun to cross-examine the prisoner, and a well-educated man promptly accepted the *rôle* of counsel for the prosecution.

" Where were you in '81 ? "

" I was in Canada."

" Where were you in '80? "

" I was in Montana."

Our real murderer, an uneducated ruffian, had come from Texas, and had honoured Oregon ever since. Something of his history was probably known to the jury.

" Where were you in '79 ? "

" I was at the University at Oxford."

A derisive cheer followed this announcement.

" You at a University, a hard-looking citizen like you! Anything else? Tell that to the marines " (or whatever represents that useful body in the West).

" Hard-looking citizen or not," said Frank, boldly, " I tell you I was there."

A bright idea seemed to strike the counsel for the prosecution.

"Well," he said; "if you were at any university you must have learnt something. What books did you read?"

"Oh," said Frank, feeling a love for the names of those authors which had never before inspired him, "Livy, Virgil, Homer, Aeschylus, Euripides, and, and——"

Looks were exchanged, and our cowboy friends began to think that there might be some mistake.

"Quote some Latin," said the counsel for the prosecution, "and you are a free man."

"Propria quæ maribus, Πολυφλοισβοιο θαλασσης."

Never did the words sound so sweet to human ear. Out of the recesses of his memory this was all he could drag to light at the moment. But that was enough. Handcuffs off, apology from the Sheriff, drinks all round; and once, at any rate, in the annals of history, an Oxford education had proved of value in the Rocky Mountains. This, roughly, as far as I can remem-

ber, was Frank's story, and I think you will
acknowledge that it was a strange experience
enough. By this time the huge Yule log was
nearly reduced to ashes, the clock `had chimed
the small hours more than once, so we reluctantly
brought our first Christmas in the Rockies to a
close. I went to bed to dream that a hoarse
voice was ordering me to throw up my hands,
but they remained glued to my side. Next that
the rope was already round my neck, and I was
ordered, on pain of instant death, to quote a
page of Racine, which, needless to say, memory
refused to recall.

The next morning the cold was simply fearful.
Morris informed Jem "that it was pretty sharp
this morning." Pretty sharp! I should think it
was. The thermometer registered 59° below zero,
or 91° of frost, and your phlegmatic Englishman
opines that "it is pretty sharp." As for me, I
tried to do some house-cleaning, and got hotache
in my hands whenever I moved away from the
fire. Mrs. M—— wisely stayed in bed and left
me to manage as best I could. The clock was

frozen on Christmas night, and stopped. Now, as I write this, the Chinook wind is blowing and it is as mild as spring.

————————

January 4th.

You say my letters don't come very regularly. I write every week; but we often don't send to the post-office for days at a time during a cold spell. Mrs. M—— has recovered, and she and I between us have got the house thoroughly cleaned; it smells so fresh and nice. I have been staining the floor of our little dressing-room, and putting up red curtains; it looks very cosy. The Chinook is still roaring away, and the snow going rapidly, the air is so soft and delicious. When I was out the other day I observed millions of little black insects on the snow; so when

I got home I suggested that the Chinook brought
these insects, and that they devoured the snow,
which accounted for its disappearance. This
observation on natural history was not received
with the respect which its originality deserved.

Mrs. F—— lent me a whole heap of books the
other day, but I've not much time for reading.
Frank and I have gone in for a course of Shake-
speare this winter, whom we cannot make Jem
appreciate; he still sticks to his Tennyson, and
such lighter stuff.

The other day a beautiful gilt-edged card came
by post, which proved to be an invitation to a
bachelor's ball in Bozeman; the committee of
management consisting of all our tradespeople;
I don't think we shall go, but it is kind of them
to ask us. Jem says that the usual practice with
regard to balls is, for every bachelor for miles
round to engage "his girl" for the evening.
He has to drive her to the ball, dance with her
all the evening, provide her with supper, and
drive her home afterwards.

January 20th.

WE are rejoicing in another cold spell and a
very heavy snowfall; as the old snow had not
half melted when the fresh fall came, the snow
is about two feet deep. To add to our misery,
everyone in the house, except me, is suffering
from what they call mountain fever. I have
doctored them all out of my medicine chest, and
hope they will soon recover.

Last time I went out, Jem took his gun and
we went scrambling about in the deep snow,
hunting for game; but only got a pheasant (something resembling a grouse more than a pheasant,
only its meat is white when cooked) and a couple
of rabbits. Suddenly Jem stopped and told me
to come up quickly; when I saw a large grey
wolf close to us, slinking away as fast as he could.
He looked an awful coward, and much afraid of
us. These large grey wolves are luckily rare, as
they do a great deal of damage amongst young
colts and calves. Government pays a bounty of, I

think, ten shillings a head for their destruction. This is the first wild animal I've seen, except antelope and white-tailed deer. I'm afraid there are no bears about here.

January 26th.

THIS week we made a huge snowball to repre-sent wickets, and made snow cricket-balls, as hard as a brick, and used my tennis racquet as a bat. Of course, we could not move about much, as the snow was so deep; still it was pretty good fun. Amusement is rather scarce just now, as the snow is so deep, and the cold too great to allow of riding or driving.

I've been trying to instil tidiness and cleanli-ness into Mrs. M——. She is very willing, but *very* dirty and untidy. One advantage of this couple is that they have been used to such poverty that they don't expect much, which is just as well out here. Still, I hope some day to be able to have rather a better class of people. We had pancakes made with snow the other day, instead of eggs; Jem pronounced them "ripping." I had heard of people making them in Russia with snow, and wanted to try them.

It's a great shame the way some people neglect their cattle out here. Those which are right back in the hills where the grass is good do well enough; but those which are down among the settlements, where feed is so scarce, ought to be fed. A small bunch of all ages, from a six months' calf to very old cows, comes past here every day. They make furious attacks on our hay corral; even barbed wire hardly stops them, and they get terribly cut trying to get through. I feel very sorry for them, but of course we can't feed them, as all the hay is wanted for our horses. What these cattle live on is a mystery. Certainly they pick over the litter which is thrown out of our stable; that and dry twigs is all they can possibly get. It will be interesting to watch if they get through the winter. If they *do*, I'm sure no one need ever be afraid of cattle not making their own living out here all the year round.

I saw in the *Field* the other day, that an English farmer had got three weeks' imprisonment for starving a cow. I shrewdly suspect that a good many Montana cattle-men would spend their whole lives in prison at that rate.

January 31st.

THE Morrises are getting very independent and troublesome; I can hardly get any work out of Mrs. M——, and 1 expect we shall have to part with them. They are talking of going, and I for one shan't miss them; I've had to show Mrs. M—— how to do everything, and generally

done the cooking myself.   Only fancy, Mrs.
F—— asked them to tea with her.   How can
anyone keep servants in their place, when the
people, whom we associate with, invite them to
their houses as equals ?

We had a delicious ride the other day.   The
weather has changed since I last wrote, and the
snow has all gone.   Jem went to buy hay, and
we rode all along by the river, jumping several
fences.   It was really good going, and reminded
one of riding over the old English pastures.   I
listened to Jem bargaining, and felt glad I don't
have anything of that kind to do.   The people
are so independent, and seem as if they would
sooner keep what they have to sell, for ever, than
take a penny less than they ask.

They generally put the price up the moment
anyone comes to buy; then when the intending
purchaser goes away disgusted, they complain
that they can't sell anything, and that there is no
money in the country.   And yet they would act
in exactly the same way if another purchaser
came the next day.

Some Englishmen, who are feeding about 300 pigs on their ranche near here, are coming down with a pig for us to-day, so we shall be well off for meat. The bullock we killed in November isn't nearly finished yet, so it has held out well. I think it is a great advantage living in a country where you can freeze your meat, and let it hang until you want it. With regard to the beef, Jem affords us a good deal of amusement. If a cold spell comes, he's miserable because it is so hard on the horses ; if a chinook comes, he's in a state of mind about the beef for fear it should go bad. So far, there seems to be no fear of that, it takes a long time to thaw out.

To-day is the first day I've seen real mud since I've been here, it seems quite home-like; which reminds one of the British tar, who, on returning to London from the Mediterranean, exclaimed, "No more of your confounded blue skies, here's a jolly old English fog."

All our young colts have been weaned, and have been kept up in the yard for the last few weeks; they are doing well, and it is a great

4

amusement to me to pet and gentle them. The mischievous little wretches are always slipping out, and getting back to their mothers; so we have to be very careful to keep the yard gate shut.

February 8th.

As we were riding up to town the other day, we saw a waggon and horses running away; so off we went as hard as we could, plunging through snowdrifts, and stumbling into badger-holes covered by the snow, to head them. After circling them round a little while, we managed to stop them. Daisy nearly ran away with me, under the impression that she was running a race. After waiting some time, a very fat old man came waddling and puffing through the snow to claim his conveyance, and was profuse in his thanks.

I wonder there are not more runaways; they are always leaving their horses standing, while they go into the saloon—or bar, as we should call it—and as they have no regular cart-horses, but all rather light, well-bred, high-lifed horses, it is surprising that they stand as well as they do.

I 've been occupying myself with dressmaking this week, turning and altering some old things, to wear when I 'm working in the mornings.

February 22nd.

ALL this week the weather has been delicious; we 've had no fires in the house until the evening, and *now* there are seven inches of snow. It is

4 *

snowing hard, and there is no sign of its
stopping.

The other day I went with Jem and Frank in
the hay-rack to get a load of hay, from a stack
about two miles from here. Going there I was
nearly shaken to death. I do think a hay-rack
is the roughest conveyance ever invented. While
they were loading up, I lay on the haystack; it
smelt delicious, like new-mown hay, and the
sun was so warm, that I only had to close
my eyes to imagine I was lying on a
haycock in the middle of summer. On the way
back we got a good many prairie-chicken. They
are not the least suspicious of a waggon, though
quite unapproachable on foot now. Frank missed
one sitting on the top of a very high tree, and it
actually sat there waiting to be shot at again,
apparently quite innocent of where the shot
came from.

A very valuable colt was running in the yard
the other day, when the stupid little thing jumped
a high half door into the stables and fell, dis-
locating its knee. None of the men could pull it in

again, so they telegraphed for the doctor from
Three Forks; he came driving at full speed and
got here at six o'clock, and quickly put the poor
little fellow right again, bandaging the knee with
plaster-of-paris.   We made the doctor stop for
dinner, but he would not stay the night; he seems
a very clever man to talk to, a Canadian, but likes
to be thought an American.   He is very well off,
and has made every penny himself.   I don't think
I should mind being doctored by him, he is so
pleasant.

On Friday, Jem and I rode nearly all day, looking for two mares, which had strayed.   We went
up into the hills.   It is the first time I have been
there.   No one can imagine how lovely it is
until they have been there; so free and such
lovely air; any number of horses, some gentle,
some wild.   We saw any amount of the Company's horses, and Jem was delighted to see them
looking so fat and well, though how they live
is a marvel to me.   The snow is still deep, but in
places there are little bare patches with short
brown grass on them (buffalo-grass Jem calls it),

which is supposed to be such wonderful stuff, and it must be, or they could not do so well on it.

The range is made up of beautiful deep valleys with streams of clear water always running; then flat plains, then more hills and high mountains beyond. When we were up there, we saw a jack rabbit (just like a Scotch hare, all white), and some antelope. We saw no traces of our two mares, but the boys found them yesterday.

March 1st.

I HAVE been out very little lately, except to go for hay in the waggon, as the ground is frightful with mud and water. One day this week I went out to see what Jem calls Sunday-school, which consists in putting a saddle on all the yearlings,

and making Johnny ride them.   One little wretch
began to buck, sent Johnny off, and kicked him
as she ran away. I think the boy will ride well
some day, as he stuck on for two or three jumps.
Then Jem got on, and there was no end of a scene;
the colt bucking and bawling all round the yard,
and doing her best to get him off; but, of course,
he was too heavy for her to buck very hard. Then
Frank came and rode one; and so they went on
for about an hour. The way these horses bawl
out here is most extraordinary; just like a cow or
a calf,—it does sound so wicked.

Our hens are beginning to lay well; we have
just built a capital hen-house of logs, laid one on
top of the other, with the chinks filled up with
mortar; so 1 hope we shall get some chickens
soon, when the warm weather comes. Our stock
of poultry consists of about thirty or forty common
barn-door fowls. The skunks and coyotes rather
interfere with the increase of the fowl population:
still I hope we may do pretty well with the
chickens—which is my department—as Jem says
this is a very good chicken ranche. The birds get

their own living all the summer in the brush, and moreover the brush protects them from the large hawks, which are very destructive to chickens on the open prairie.

I think I told you that our ranche was down on the river bottom, all amongst the trees and brush. This country is quite destitute of such ornaments, except on the river bottoms, though the high mountains are covered with a dense growth of pines.

The worst of chicken-farming here is, that in summer there is a glut of eggs, when they only fetch about sixpence a dozen, and are hard to sell even at that price, and the winters are, of course, too cold to allow hens to lay at all. However, eggs will be very useful in summer, when it is most difficult to have any fresh meat, as it will not keep more than a day or two, and out here you have to get such a quantity at a time. It will be nice here in summer when all the trees are out, and if we can make a lawn round the house it will be very pretty. At present I'm afraid English people would be much astonished at the mess round the house. In winter, of course, nothing can be done on account of the snow.

March 15th.

The weather is perfect now. We have tea out of doors, on the garden seat, in front of the house. I've been riding every day, and everything seems to be enjoying the warm weather; all the horses are getting sleek and fat, you never saw such a difference.

We have begun breakfast at 7.30, which Mrs. M—— seems to think a great grievance, and has been in a very bad temper in consequence; so I told her if we had any more of her temper she would have to go; this threat seems to have had a good effect.

The hens are beginning to lay well, any amount

of eggs; I find them in all sorts of queer places. My worst enemies are the magpies, who steal such numbers. They seem to know what the cackling of a hen means, as well as I do.

Jem and Frank are busy in the evenings making a fence all round the house, enclosing about two acres. This is to be the fruit and flower garden, at present we have nothing in it but rhubarb. Nearly all the old rubbish has been cleared away, and they are planning out paths and a drive, which is to be laid down in gravel. We can get plenty of that from the river. We expect to make our Home Farm of 160 acres pay for our living and domestics; but, of course, our main-stay is the horse business.

All the spring birds are arriving, so spring will soon be here, I hope. I saw some robins to day, which are like the English birds, only much larger, as big as blackbirds; and I also saw some beautiful blue birds—these only come here in the spring and summer.

March 23rd.

THERE was an eclipse of the sun to-day; the result of which was, that it got pitch dark about 10 A.M., remained so for three-quarters of an hour and blew a hurricane all the time.

I'm going into the stock business on my own account and mean to invest in a cow, as Polly has gone dry. I find it almost impossible to make puddings without milk or butter, even though we do have plenty of eggs. The South Kensington book is very useful, as there are so many simple recipes in it.

We are getting lots of little pigs now, and hope they will prove profitable. Pork has been worth 5d. a pound till this year, but, I suppose, like everything else, it will go down in price soon. Mrs. M—— is getting so fine, that she grumbles at having to eat pork, and thinks beef is to be got as easily as it is in England. Jem says Mrs. M—— won't eat pork because the pigs had been fed on horse-flesh. She got this idea into her head because the Englishmen, who are feeding 300 pigs, gave some of theirs a lot of dead horses which were smothered in a closed railway truck.

The man who shipped them put twenty in a closed truck, and eighteen of them were smothered before they had gone fifteen miles. They were thrown out close to the pig ranche, and were a great find for the pig-feeders. You know I told you we got a pig from there, and so Mrs. M—— got the idea into her head that this pig had been fed on horse-flesh. If pigs never ate anything worse than good fresh horse-flesh, I, for one, should not mind. The other morning Mrs. M—— brought a piece of pork with a piece of string stuck in it, and assured me, with a long face, that this pig must have been " fed upon string."

Now that the ice is out of the river, we catch plenty of fish. The bait is generally a bit of raw meat; they won't take a fly yet. There are three kinds of fish in our river and " creek "— trout, grayling, and white fish. The latter are very unsuspicious and easily caught, but not half as good eating as either of the former, and don't give half as good sport (when you are fishing for sport), as they give in directly they are hooked, and you pull them out as if they were dead. When we are not fishing for sport, but only for the pot, we use a long stick and a piece of strong line, with a bit of raw meat on the hook, and jerk the fish out right over our heads as soon as they bite. It is not very sportsman-like, but very effective and expeditious.

I've been helping Jem to "fix up" fences. They use what are called "snake" fences a good deal out here, which are made without any posts, by simply laying poles one over the other. They are called "snake" fences because they don't go straight, but form an angle, where the poles overlap each other, but I thought that they had that name because they were built so that snakes could not get through.

March 29th.

WE tried a new "buggy" mare the other day, and she behaved very well; trotted ten miles in an hour, and only astonished us once by kicking, and that was only play, as she was fresh and evidently enjoyed being out.   Jem thinks she's going to make a trotter.

They think more of a trotter out here than anything else, and often astonish me by saying Daisy is too good for a "saddle horse," and would make such a good " buggy " animal. Too good for a saddle horse ! That seems to be rather upsetting the order of things, according to English notions at least.   But here they seem to think anything is good enough to ride, and that the pick of the flock ought to be kept for harness. It seems to me that one might define the Americans as a " driving " race.

A revolution has taken place in our establishment. The Morrises leave on Tuesday, if they can find a place to go to.   I could not stand her

any longer. Latterly, if I have dared to say a
word as to what work she ought to do, or ventured to say the potatoes were not boiled, or
anything of that sort, she has flown into a pas-
sion, and broken out into the "unshackled
Doric" of Battersea. They have both got very
independent, and say that, in this country, people
won't be "hired servants." I shan't miss her
much, as I've had to do most things myself
lately, and we shall get our washing done by
the Chinaman in Moreland for 25s. a month.
Morris is going on working on the farm at £9
a month, and will board and lodge himself. I
shall enjoy the extra work immensely, and shall
feel as if I really was living in the Far West,
doing everything for myself. Won't it be a
blessing never to have the bother of servants?

This whole upset has really been caused by
the neighbours, who are so jealous of anyone
having servants, as they don't have them themselves; so they have been telling the Morrises
that it is *infra dig.* for a white man to be a
"hired servant," and how much better they can

do on their own account, telling them they ought to have their meals with us and sit in the drawing-room, and so on. Therefore, they have become discontented, ill-tempered, and utterly unbearable.

April 8th.

WE are having a most exciting time of it. The Morrises left on Tuesday. After I had seen them safely off the premises, I saddled up Daisy, and rode down towards Three Forks to meet Jem. I rode nearly half way without meeting him ; then had to turn back for a new reason, viz. to cook dinner. Just as I got back to town I was hailed by a great big man with a beard, dressed in white leathers and jack-boots, so I knew he was an Englishman. He exclaimed " How do you do, Mrs. ——? You do not know me." I recognized the voice, but it was some time before I made out the features of Mr. M——, an old friend, under the disguise of a beard. Then Mr. J——, another Englishman whose acquaintance we had made in the train coming out, came up and shook hands with me.

My first thought was, "Is there enough dinner?" and then I asked them to come down, and here they are now. I get through the work and the cooking well, and give them English dinners every night—soup, meat, and pudding—and the men all help me to wash up afterwards. Jem, Frank, and I are all pretty busy now, as we have all the domestic duties to perform, besides the boys' ordinary work. We get up at 6 o'clock, Jem lights the fire, whilst I'm dressing. I cook breakfast, which has to be pretty substantial for four hungry men, while Jem and Frank go out and do the stables, milk the cow, &c. Our guests are very good and help too. For breakfast we have porridge (which Americans call "mush"), eggs, fried potatoes, and cold

5

game or meat of some kind, not to mention
the "hot biscuits," as they are called out here—
breakfast rolls, you would call them; mine, I
assure you, are excellent, and the boys seem to
think so too.

One afternoon, while Mr. J—— and Mr. M——
were with us, they said I wanted a holiday; so
Frank, who is a capital cook, offered to get dinner
ready for us by the time we got back. Accordingly, the rest of us rode off in high glee,
and had a jolly cross-country ride, to look at a
band of horses which Jem thought would suit
Mr. J——, who had come to our country to buy
horses. I rode Daisy, of course, and Mr. M——
rode a half-sister of Daisy's for the first time.
He fell in love with her (so did I), and offered
Jem £40 for her, which is considered a pretty
good price in this country, but Jem says she
is worth double that price in the Eastern
markets.

When we got back, hungry and happy, about
7 o'clock, we found Frank had a regular banquet
ready for us: bean soup, fresh-caught trout,

haunch of venison with buffalo-berry jelly, compôte of (dried) apples, *and* a beautiful sponge cake, made with nothing but flour, water, sugar, and eggs. When we had done ample justice to his good things we washed up, went into the drawing-room, and, lighting a bright wood fire, the men sat round it, pipe in mouth, in great comfort.

I went to the piano, and soon somebody suggested a song. Mr. J——, who sang very well, gave us "The Place where the Old Horse died," and he and Mr. M—— sang a duet, "Annie Laurie." Frank, after much pressing, sang Besant's rather melancholy ditty out of "Uncle Jack," beginning "The ship was outward bound, when we drank a health around." But Frank's rendering, to a tune of his own, and playing his accompaniment with one finger, was killing. When he came to the line, "One in far Alaska pioneering died," his feelings nearly overcame him, and we thought he wept. Jem gave us the "The Bicester Hunt," and so we went on with song and anecdote till midnight. A thoroughly jolly evening.

5 *

Next day the men all rode up to the horse ranche, except Mr. M——, whom I drove in the buggy. The "round-up," was going on, and there were about 300 horses in the corral. You never saw such a scene. Men brandishing clubs, whooping and yelling, more like wild Indians than civilized beings. Horses (they were nearly all wild) rushing from one side of the corral to the other, all huddled together and terrified to death. Well they might be! I'm sure I could not make out what the men wanted them to do, and so I don't see how the poor wretched horses could. Whenever a horse came out of the bunch he was immediately headed back, with shouts, yells, and blows from clubs.

At last, however, I noticed that some were allowed to come by, and were passed through into another corral. Then I found out that they were trying to separate the different brands. Each owner has his own brand, and they cut out all belonging to A., branded with a triangle, for instance, and A. takes his horses off ; then B. gets his, and so on, until they are all separated. They seem to be very rough, and what with men, and especially boys, wild with excitement, and horses with terror, they make mad work of it.

———————

April 16th.

OUR visitors have just left us, to our great regret, after a jolly visit of a fortnight. We sent them up to the station, with Daisy's half-sister in the buggy for the first time. She behaved very badly, and one of them had to lead her the whole way. However, she took their things up. The weather was lovely during the whole fortnight, and we were able to sit with our windows open all day. Mr. J——, who is a large cattle-owner, and is therefore not bothered with any small matters like pigs and poultry, observing all the things we have to do now that we have no servants, justly remarked, "Verily it is a life

of toil." And so it is; still, we are all very
happy, which is the main thing.

I think our visitors enjoyed themselves. Mr.
J——, who has not been home for years, said how
nice it was to meet a lady again, and sit in an
English-looking drawing-room, with some of the
refinements of life.

I am wearing summer clothes, and the prairie
is green and gorgeous with flowers, especially a
little white flower, which grows in bunches and
smells delicious. Besides my usual work indoors,
I have been painting the garden palings green
and washing windows, which latter I find I can
do better than I expected.

I'm so thankful to be rid of Mrs. M——. At
all events, I can keep the house clean now, and
it is easier to do it myself than it was to make
her do it. Jem and Frank say that they live
much better, and now we know that everything
we eat is clean, which is more than we did
before. I don't want to be bothered with any
more servants if I can possibly manage to do
without them; it is no use trying to have

them out here; even *good* English ones would be spoilt in a month. The natives are very queer, independent, and rough; it is no use trying to make them into *servants*, and very disagreeable to have half-educated, ill-mannered sort of people to eat and sit with you; and if you had English ones, the natives would soon make them discontented.

I must say one thing. I think the men about here have very good manners, and are always very nice to me. The men who work at the horse ranche all take their hats off to me; not at all because I am the wife of their employer, but because they seem to know that it is good manners to take their hats off to a lady. Jem says they would never dream of taking their hats off to him if I wasn't with him, or showing any other token of respect.

April 25th.

THIS last week we have had cold storms of rain and snow; however, we don't mind, as it does so much good to the grass and crops.

Yesterday Jem and I made a great excursion to a ranche about ten miles off to fetch a pig. When we arrived there the man looked at me as I sat in the buggy holding the reins, and said "Won't the woman come in?" Jem smiled, but declined with thanks.

He says that "the woman" is the common term for a man's wife out here. At the same time he says that if he is talking of any female to the natives, and remarks, "What a nice woman Mrs. So-and-so is," they always reply, "Yes, she's a very nice *lady*," with a great stress on the *lady*.

In a few minutes Jem and the man appeared, carrying the pig. We put it in a sack and laid it at our feet, and it took up all the room at the bottom of the buggy. Before we had gone very far I nearly pitched Jem out by driving too fast over a ditch, both his hands being occupied with holding the pig in. Piggy got his nose out and wanted to bite, uttering the most frightful squeals, which frightened our horse out of his wits. Then down came a frightful storm of wind, rain, and hail. Our hands were nearly frozen, as I had to hold the reins, and Jem the pig. However, after numerous shaves of upsetting the buggy, and determined, but ineffectual, efforts to escape on the part of the pig, we got home safely. Then Jem and I had to lift piggy out bodily, hoist him over some palings, and drop him into the stye. Altogether it was most ludicrous, and, except for the cold and wet, great fun.

I can't tell you what a blessing it is to have got rid of Mrs. M——. You can't imagine the mess I found everything in after she had gone. The house has kept twice as clean ever since. Luckily my men are both very tidy and good about wiping their boots, &c. I generally get through my work by 1 o'clock (breakfasting at 7.15), and have the dinner all ready and half cooked by that time, so

that I need not have much to do in the afternoon.
There is the kitchen stove to clean; but wood
leaves clean ashes. Frank lights the fires for me
in the morning. I find I get through my work
with very little trouble after all, as I have a certain time fixed for everything, and cook particular
things on certain days. I always give them "hot
biscuits" for breakfast, fried potatoes, eggs, pork,
or bacon, beef, or fish cakes. The cooking I
really enjoy, and invent all kinds of new dishes.
My sponge cakes rival Frank's for lightness, and
I make plenty of pastry and apple tarts.

No fruit is grown in this country at present,
so we use "evaporated" or dried fruit, which is
cooked like Normandy pippins. The dried fruit,
reminds me of the sheep-herder's remark about
Montana, when he got up on the 1st July, to
find a snowstorm raging : "Confounded country,
where it snows every month in the year, and
dried apples are a luxury."

One does feel rather like that one-self, when
the weather is bad. There's nothing small about
the climate here : when it's good, it's *very* good;

and when it's bad, it *is* bad. Luckily the good very much predominates.

We took the washing up to John Chinaman for the first time, this week, and found him doing his hair, which he makes into one long plait, and then coils round his head like a crown. He seemed very good-natured, kept on grinning and saying, " Ah ! " " Yah ! " but I could not understand a word he said.

May 1st.

THE prairies are simply lovely, quite covered with flowers ; pink and white ox-eyed daisies in tiny round bunches, growing quite close to the ground (none of the flowers here have any stalks), yellow flowers (called prickly pear, really a sort of cactus), small pansies, lenten lilies, and many others. The air is literally scented with them all.

We went to Bozeman this week, to buy curtains, carpet, etc., for one of the up-stairs rooms ; as a young Englishman is coming out to stay with us. I don't think I ever explained to you how many rooms there are in our house, and what the house is like.

In the first place, there is the new part of the house, two storeys high, consisting of hall, our bed-room and sitting room on each side of the hall, and up-stairs two bed-rooms. Then there is the old part of the house, immediately behind and joined on to the new part, consisting of three cabins in a row, all joined together, and beyond them a stone dairy. A door opens from the hall into the dining-room, and from the dining-room you go straight through another door into the kitchen (which has another door opening into the garden) and from the kitchen through another door into Jem's den. The up-stairs rooms are plastered and whitewashed; but the drawing-room, our bed-room, the hall, and Jem's den are papered;

the dining-room and kitchen walls are boarded
and painted. The new two-storey part of the
house is built of carefully-hewn logs, stained
brown, and looks rather nice ; the old part is of
unhewn logs. The roof is all made of shingles
(*i.e.* pieces of wood sawn thin and resembling
slates). We have seven good-sized rooms, besides
the hall, our small dressing-room and the dairy.
They say when this house was built, about fifteen
or sixteen years ago, it was *the* show house of the
country. Since then, of course, a great many
better houses have been built, but ours is very
comfortable and quite good enough for this
country. I believe it cost the original owner
about £500, but we bought the farm, 160 acres,
stables, house, and everything as it stood, so it is
impossible to say what such a house would cost
now. All we've done in the way of building is
a new stable, a yard in the shape of a quadrangle,
with sheds all round, and the stone dairy, and
divers out-houses, pig-styes, chicken-house, &c.
From our experience of this, building is still a
very expensive amusement, and I think it would

always be cheaper to buy a ranche already well improved, than to do any building oneself.

May 16th.

THIS week Frank started off to the hills, with a tent and waggon and supplies for a month, to start a new ranche up in the mountains as a summer ranche for our horses. He took another man with him, and we expect he will be gone for a month at least. Our English friend also arrived this week, but does not seem to like the life, so I'm afraid he won't stay long with us.

Jem and I went a long ride into the hills north of us, on the other side of the river, to look for a mare and four yearlings, which have strayed off our range. We started at eight, and did not get home until seven. I was rather stiff and tired, but I was riding the laziest horse on the ranche, such a brute, it was almost as hard work to get him along as to walk.

May 31st.

LAST night we were all sitting in Jem's den reading the English papers when I heard Noble (an imported Shire horse) kicking in his box—he has a trick of rolling, and sometimes gets fast and can't get up—so I told Jem I heard him kicking, and, while he was pulling on his boots, I looked out of the window, which faces the stable, and, to my horror, saw the stables in flames! We all rushed out at once; but though Jem opened the door of Noble's box and the horse came out, he was either already badly burnt, or suffocated with the smoke; for he only staggered out and immediately fell backwards into the flames and died without a struggle. It was horrible. Noble was such a good horse, and everyone was so fond of him.

The flames spread with frightful rapidity; the buildings being all wood and all in one block, there was no hope of saving anything from the first. We did all we could, getting out saddles, harness and everything we could lay our hands on. Luckily there were no other horses in the stables that night; but one was bad enough, as, apart from our being so fond of him, Noble was worth twenty ordinary horses. The people up in town saw the flames, and came rushing down; but nothing could be done. In half an hour from the time when I first saw the flames, everything was burnt to the ground: all our implements, buggy, and hundreds of odd things were completely destroyed. We were all working hard until two o'clock in the morning, putting out the fire, which had caught dead branches in the trees.

Two cowboys, whom Jem had known for a long time, stayed all night and until quite late next morning, carrying pails of water to pour on the red-hot ashes and smouldering timbers, for fear the wind should get up and blow sparks from them on to the house. It was most fortunate that the wind was not blowing towards the house last night, or *it* must have gone too. Jem and I are still carrying pails of water to put out the ashes; but the danger is over now, I think.

The whole place looks most wretched; all the trees round the house and stables burnt, and nothing but a heap of ashes and blackened timbers to show where all our beautiful buildings stood. It is most melancholy to see the saddle horses, &c. come trooping up to be fed. They seem quite lost at having no stables to go into, and, of course, there are no oats or hay to feed them with. The chickens, most of which we saved, and the pigs, are also wandering about disconsolate; altogether, it is most piteous. Of course, we shall have to abandon the idea of our summer ranche in the mountains now, as we must build up this one again.

A few days after the fire, the A——s, English

people living near here, came over to luncheon.
Mrs. A—— has just come out from England, and
it is so nice to have someone of one's own sex
to talk to again. I gave them a grand luncheon,
and hope we shall see a great deal of them, as
their place is only about fifteen miles from here,
just a nice ride to luncheon and back again. Just
as they were starting home, Mr. J—— turned up
again, and stayed a few days with us; of course
we were delighted to see him, as he is always so
cheery.

———

June 6th.

JEM and Frank are hard at work irrigating the
crops, wheat and peas. They can't find a man
to do it, so they are trying to do it themselves.
It seems very interesting work; they fill the

different ditches with water, then dam them up at
the highest point, cut a hole in one of the banks,
and let the water run out on to the land on
both sides of the ditch. Nothing will grow
here without irrigation. All this keeps Jem
very busy, as he is manager of the Company's
horse herd, and has to look after that in addition to his work at home.

Half my time, whilst I'm writing this, is taken
up with fighting mosquitoes; they are getting
bad now. At night, when we are sitting out in
the garden, it is so curious watching the fire-
flies flitting in and out of the trees and bushes.
The first time I saw them I thought there must
be a fire somewhere, and those were the sparks.
The nights are getting rather hot now. We
generally get up at 4.30 in the morning; I do
the house, cooking, &c., and then every day last
week I either rode up in the hills with Jem,
drove our horses down to the Horse Ranche, or
else I rode Daisy, going errands for Jem.

I went down to the " Pig " Ranche yesterday,
and heard that they were thinking of selling

6 *

their ranche to an Englishman, *and his wife*. So, you see, we shall have quite a colony of English ladies out here soon; however, I can claim the credit of being the pioneer. The principal flowers out now are the wild rose and single sunflower; they grow in profusion.

June 14th.

I've been having a pretty lively week of it. Jem started for Helena on Monday, eighty miles, on horseback, and isn't back yet. I haven't heard anything about him, though I expected him back yesterday. He went to buy a horse to replace poor old Noble. Frank also went on Monday to hunt horses, and I'm all alone in my glory; not quite though, as we have a young

Englishman, fresh from the old country, staying with us.

On Tuesday morning, the latter wanted to go to the " Pig " Ranche to borrow some tennis balls, so I saddled and bridled my little " cayuse " (or cow pony) which I always keep picketed, and started out with a huge long whip (our gentle mares are such wretches, they stand still and kick at you instead of going on, when you want to drive them anywhere ; so you have to use a whip) to find our horses. After plunging through swamps and brush for some time, I found them all, drove them home and corralled them all by myself. Then I caught our friend's horse, saddled and bridled it for him, and having walked a quarter of a mile to open a gate for him, I went home to enjoy my own company for the day.

He came back in the evening, bringing the balls, and we had some grand games of tennis. We had rolled a place up on the flat ; it was pretty rough and uneven, but good enough for us to enjoy playing. We cut two poles from a tree, and stuck up some wire netting, and marked out the

ground with whitewash ; unfortunately, we didn't
get the corners quite square, but it didn't matter
much.   Harry (Jem's cousin) came down, and I
got him to stay the night. Next day Mr. H——,
another Englishman, appeared, directly after
breakfast, and when I had done my work, we
played tennis all day.

Suddenly we saw someone else coming, and, lo
and behold ! it was Mr. M—— turned up again !
He only stayed one day, being on his way to England. I must say I envied him. Frank came
back last night, not having found the horses
which he went to look for. To-day we all spent
in making a fence to keep the pigs off the peas.
Before we had finished breakfast, down came Mr.
H—— to see us. He told me a lot of news. People
do gossip out here, *and* quarrel. There were " six-
shooters " out up at the Hotel the other evening—
a terrible row going on; of course everyone had
been drinking this disgusting whisky. It's rather
exciting hearing about it afterwards, but they say
whisky is the curse of this country.

Frank and I were playing tennis yesterday,

when the man, who is hauling lumber for our new
stables, came by. He stopped and gazed, then
said, "Having a game of ball?" He grinned
and seemed to think it a great joke. When we
had finished, we met him coming back, and he
said to Frank, "I guess you let the lady win."
He wanted to know if it was an amusement. They
are funny people. We've got a man working for
us now, who is a tremendous talker; since Jem
has been away, whenever I show my nose anywhere near him, he calls out, "Say Mrs.", and then
asks me my opinion about the stables, &c., and
boasts of what a splendid building he is going to
make. I must tell you that all the natives think
that our tennis ground is the ground plan for our
new stables. The white lines puzzled them ex-
ceedingly, but that is the solution they always
arrive at. Oh! the people here have a high
opinion of themselves, and tell pretty good yarns;
one never believes more than a quarter of what
they say.

I'm sorry to say that the woman, who used to
come once a week to scrub floors, can't come any

more, so I shall have to learn. I daresay it isn't
so hard as it looks. I wish one or two of the
girls I know, who complain of having nothing to
do at home, would come out here. They would
find plenty to do, and amusement too.

———————

June 23rd.

JEM came back last Tuesday, having been away
over a week. He brought back a beautiful big
black horse, but not so good a horse as Noble, we
think, though everyone else is in raptures about
him. Jem bought a band of mares when he was
away, and stopped the night at the A——'s, next
day there was a regular procession, Jem leading his
big horse in front, then a band of about twenty
mares and colts, and then Mrs. A—— and her

brother driving them.   They lunched here, and
rode home in the evening.

One day last week we took a holiday, and rode
down to spend the day with them.   It was very
hot riding, and in some places the mosquitoes
were terrible.   They literally covered our horses,
until we could hardly see what colour they were.
I am getting nearly devoured, but I console myself by thinking that next year I shan't mind
these pests.   They always bite people worse the first
year.   We had a very jolly day with the A——'s,
and got back here at 11 P.M.   It was deliciously
cool riding back in the evening.   Major A——
congratulated me on having a holland habit, and
thought it looked so cool.   I never wear a habit
at all about home, neither does Mrs. A——.

I was left all alone the other day, as Jem and
Frank were both hunting horses a long way off,
in different directions.   When it began to get
dark, I shut all the doors, put chairs against them,
and then departed to bed.   Luckily I never think
of robbers out here, so I was quite happy.   I
woke up in the middle of the night, hearing Jem

coming down the hill, singing "Some Day" to let me know who it was, so that I mightn't be alarmed. It was just one o'clock, and he had ridden, I don't know how many miles, so as not to leave me alone.

Our new stables are being put up. They are much smaller than the old ones, but we hope to improve them some day. My bread has just risen, so I must finish this and attend to it. I not only have to make my own bread out here, but my own yeast, which is made with potatoes and hops, and old yeast to make it ferment. I have to make it very often in summer, as it so soon goes sour.

July 12th.

IT is getting dreadfully hot now. They say July and August are the two hottest months in the year, just as January and February are the coldest. There are thunder-storms nearly every afternoon. They are much more violent here than they are in England, but then everything in this country is on a large scale. I am getting quite a useful hand on the ranche. I have ridden out alone in the hills several times this week, *I do like it so.* It is so nice riding to all the different bunches of horses which I see in the distance, studying the brands, and then, when I come to those I want, cutting them out, and driving them down to the ranche. The horse I ride seems to enjoy the whole thing too. I use a cow-pony for this work, as Daisy is too excitable. My being able to do all this, saves Jem lots of time, as he and Frank are very busy just now farming and irrigating.

We had hired a man to work by the month at £9 a month to do this; but when our stables and everything were burnt, we set him to build a new stable. He got so elated with his skill as a carpenter, that he went up to town one day and said "it wasn't likely that a first-rate *mechanic* was going to work for only £9 a month!" He never came to work any more, and it was only by accident that we learnt the reason. He never told us that he was going to leave, but quietly left us in the lurch, just at the busy time, when it is quite impossible to find anyone else; so the boys made up their minds to turn farm-hands themselves. Though they are quite at home when it comes to handling stock, I don't know what kind of farmers they'll make. I think gentlemen generally make better stockmen than farm-hands, but, of course, out here men have to do anything that turns up.

On Thursday, after I had done my work, I started off at 8 o'clock to Three Forks, riding Daisy, and leading another horse. I had to go slowly all the way, as the other horse led so

badly and kept pulling back, which nearly drove
Daisy frantic, and started her "bucking" a
little.   However, I managed to stick on her and
not let the other horse go.   I lunched with the
A——s, and saw all the other English people down
there.   Soon after I had started home a terrific
thunder-storm came on.   Luckily there was a
ranche about a mile farther on (American), so I
galloped on there as fast as I could, jumped the
fence in front of the house, to the great astonishment of the natives, and asked for shelter.   I
stayed there chatting until the storm was over.
The people were very pleasant.   But the house!
You can't imagine anything dirtier—only two
rooms in it.   The room we sat in had no carpet,
and *such* a dirty floor; no furniture except a deal
table, two wooden chairs, and a rough bunk
covered with blankets, which answered the pur-
pose of a sofa by day and bed by night.   There
was nothing like the comfort which you would
see in a farm-labourer's cottage at home, and
yet these people were well off.

When the storm was over, I trotted on, but

had not gone far when down came the rain in sheets, so I galloped about three miles further, and got to the Pig Ranche, went in there, and found the owners at home. They luckily had a fire in the kitchen, so I dried my dripping garments and helped them to cook supper, which I afterwards also helped to eat. Then I rode home in the dark, and found the boys quietly smoking in front of the house, imagining that I was safely at Three Forks.

The A——s came over on Saturday to stay the night, and we had a very jolly evening, songs and music. Mrs. A—— made such a pretty sketch of the house, which I will send you. We are going to try and get a holiday soon, and hope to start on my birthday. We are going up into the mountains, and shall take all our gentle mares and colts up with us. Then we can leave home happily, knowing that they won't be stolen in our absence. The boys hope to have done irrigating, and won't have much to do until the crops are cut. I saw H—— up in town to-day, and he looked so miserably ill, that I asked him to come down and rest until he was well. He has got a touch of mountain fever.

July 28th.

WE have been busy haymaking all this week. It is a very nice job here, as it is cut, and raked up into rows, cocked (with the horse-rake) and carried all in the same day. I drove the hay-rake all one day. It was quite a luxury driving, sitting on a high spring-seat, and pulling up and letting down the lever constituted carriage exercise. Perhaps if people tried horse-raking when they are ordered carriage exercise, they would get a little of the latter. We have done all our hay without any help, only Jem and Frank and myself. Jem has just been in to say that if I

can come now he will help me to pick peas, so a
good offer must not be refused. We have about
twenty acres of peas to feed the pigs in winter.
At present we are the pigs, as we live on green
peas, fish, eggs, and milk. Meat won't keep a
day in this weather; besides, it's too hot to eat
meat. The shooting season begins on August 1st,
so we shall get plenty of game then.

————————

August 2nd.

I AM writing from Three Forks: Jem
had to drive a bunch of horses to a ranche
near here, so I came to help him, and we
stopped the night with the A——s. We are
going home at 4 o'clock in the morning, so as to

ride while it is cool. The heat has been awful all this week; the thermometer has been up to 109 in the shade, and never lower than 96. What it must have been in the sun I don't know. Frank was quite knocked up by it one morning, and had to come in and lie down, and Jem was as bad another day. I haven't felt it yet quite so bad, though I've been riding in the sun most days.

On Tuesday we hope to be off to the mountains for a week's holiday, taking our waggon, tent, and camp outfit. It will be delicious to get up to the mountains, where it is cool, and do nothing but shoot and fish and lie about in the shade. I am to have a complete holiday, as Frank has promised to do the cooking, and there will be no house to clean. It really will seem, too, as if one was out in a wild country.

August 19th.

I COULD not write last Sunday, as we were
in camp up in the mountains. We started on
Thursday, driving about forty head of horses
with us. Jem and I rode and drove the horses,
and Frank went on in front with the waggon,
taking the tent, canteen, and ammunition. The
first day we went about twenty miles, and
camped by a spring of delicious cold water.

It was so jolly camping out. Frank made a
fire on the ground, and cooked frying-pan bread,
made of flour, water, and baking-powder. You
fill the frying-pan with dough, put it on the fire
until the bottom is done, and then toss it in the
air to turn it and bake the other side. It isn't
half bad bread. We had bacon, eggs, and coffee
for supper. It all tasted so good after our ride.
It was perfectly delicious at night sitting round

the camp-fire, breathing the beautiful fresh air, scented with the perfumed smoke from the logs of smouldering cedar, and looking up at the clear sky, studded with millions of stars, flashing in all their glory; not a sound to be heard except what was made by our horses busily cropping the short sweet grass, or the murmuring of our voices, softened by the pleasing languor of slight fatigue, disturbed now and then by the melancholy howl of a distant coyote. So we sat and talked of everything under the sun, until at last we got to hunting, and a comparison between the delights of the chase at home and abroad, and I think our vote was in favour of the former, bigoted Britons that we are. Then someone asked Jem about that story of the bear and the fusee.

"That reminds me," said Jem, "smoking saved that hero's life; so I'll just light my pipe in grateful memory."

Suiting the action to the word, he took an ember from the fire, puffed volumes of smoke for a few minutes, and began.

7 *

"You recollect Jack B——. Well, though there *is* a temptation to some minds to draw the long bow with regard to snakes and bears, yet I don't think that Jack was given that way, and I believe that his story, though strange, was true.

"It seems he was hunting down in Wyoming somewhere, and desperate keen on bears. So one fine morning he dropped on to an old she-bear with cubs—not exactly the most amiable creature to meet at the best of times. However, Jack didn't often miss; so, after a quick look for a handy tree in case of accidents, up went the express. The crack of the rifle produced a yell from Madame Bruin, but no other result, except a very lively movement in the direction of Master Jack, who, on his side, made an equally lively one in the direction of the tree, which he gained with very little to spare, and a very creepy feeling about his extremities, as he dragged himself into a place of safety, minus his gun.

"'Here's a go!' communed our friend, 'I'm up a tree with a vengeance, and, to make matters worse, a raging she-bear underneath. Well, I believe I'll take a smoke, and look this business square in the eye.'

"Accordingly he filled his pipe, and struck a fusee to light it. Just for fun, he dropped the fusee on Madame Bruin's back. As soon as it burnt through the hair, she jumped as if she was shot, then she rolled and growled, and bit at her back, and went on like a mad thing, until the match cooled down, when she returned to the tree, foaming at the mouth, her eyes like hot coals, and began tearing at the tree, while making violent endeavours to get on level terms with her persecutor. A few more fusees deftly dropped at intervals only served to make her madder and madder; and Jack's face grew longer and longer. He began to think which was the stronger feeling in a bear, rage or hunger, and hoped it was the latter.

"Just then the bear came open-mouthed at him, and, standing on her hind legs, did her level best to reach him. Into the red mouth of the bear dropped a red-hot fusee. Jack said her face was a picture. She holloa'ed, she rolled, she foamed, and at last she ran; just as hard as legs could carry her, she scuttled off into the brush. Jack's medicine had settled her.

"So you see," said Jem, knocking the ashes out of his pipe, "there's some good in smoking, after all, and I'll smoke another pipe on the strength of it. A pipe never does go so well as round a camp-fire. Throw another log on, Frank, like a good fellow, and we'll smoke one more pipe and turn in. By-the-bye, did I ever tell you about Colonel H—— and his patent cartridges? They must have been some left over from a Government contract, but no matter. He was hunting bear somewhere near Clark's Fork, I think, and one day he tracked a bear for a good while, and, just as he caught sight of the critter, he disappeared into a cave.

"The Colonel didn't like to be beat. It was bear he was hunting, and bear he wanted; so up he went to the cave, down he went on his hands and knees, and looked in. First of all he couldn't see a thing. At last he saw something like two red-hot coals.

" ' Ah!' thinks the Colonel, ' I 've got you ; but if I don't shoot straight, you 'll get me. You 've backed into the cave, and you can't get any further in, and you can't get out, unless I do. Well, here goes.'

" He drew a bead on that bear, and aimed steady and true right between the red-hot coals, pulled the trigger, and—click !

" ' Missed fire, by Jove ! '

" He kept his eye on those two red-hot coals, and they got bigger. He didn't dare to move, he didn't dare to breathe. He had one barrel left, and he thought he would keep that until the hot coals grew larger ; if he missed this time, he was done. It wasn't altogether nice, but he waited. At last the hot coals stopped.

" ' Now is my chance,' says the Colonel ; and he took a long, steady aim.

" Click ! Missed fire again. The Colonel said, when he heard that ' click,' he thought he could feel for a man on trial for his life, when the jury says ' Guilty.' He didn't move a muscle, but kept his eyes on the red-hot coals. Bigger and bigger they grew; nearer and nearer they came; and he thought it was all over. At last they stopped. He supposed they were stationary for a few seconds, but it seemed to him as if it was for hours. Then they moved. Thank heaven! they grew less; he breathed again. They disappeared altogether; still he dared not move. He knelt there motionless, it seemed to him, for hours.

"At last he thought he'd chance it; he could not stay there for ever. So he got up, and moved cautiously backwards, with his eye on the cave. Then he made a circle round the place, and found that there was a back entrance to the cave, and Bruin was gone. You bet, there wasn't a happier man in Wyoming that minute than Colonel H——. He went back to camp, opened his cartridges, and they were loaded with—sawdust! He opened the whole lot, and found the same harmless material in them all. He concluded to load his own cartridges for the future. These he had bought ready loaded in New York."

"That will do," says Frank, "give him the kettle."

But this was a true bill all the same.

"Well," says Jem, "you are getting sceptical; let's turn in, or I shall be spinning you bear stories until daylight."

In a few minutes we were sleeping the sleep of the weary, as if there wasn't such a thing as a rattle-snake in the world. We heard afterwards, that a man camping here a few weeks before had killed five of those charming creatures on this very spot.

Next morning, as we were boiling coffee, watching grouse frying, and warming our hands over the camp-fire, we saw a man come riding into camp with something behind his saddle. Deer would not be in season for about a week; but deer it was. Jem and Frank began chaffing the hunter about killing deer out of season.

"Well," he said, "you see, I ran across this blessed critter, and was so close to him that he got scared, didn't look where he was going, ran his head against a rock, and broke his neck; so I had to bring him along, you see."

I was just going to exclaim, "What an extraordinary thing," when I observed a sly twinkle in Frank's eye, and desisted.

"Had any more of that kind of luck?" said Frank.

"Well, no, not exactly, but one did attack me the other day, and I had to kill him in self-defence. They are dangerous at times."

As accidents will happen and a man must defend his life when attacked, we didn't refuse a shoulder of venison, in return for our grouse and coffee, even though deer *were* out of season.

After breakfast we packed up the camp outfit, started off again, and did twenty miles leisurely, and got into camp about four o'clock. We picketed two horses, pitched our tent, cooked supper, and, after a careful search for rattle-snakes turned in. Our drive took us up and down some frightful places, as we camped high up in the mountains, at least 6,000 feet above the level of the sea.

The country was perfectly lovely up there, just under the timber line, and the grass was up to our horses' knees. The scenery was something wonderful. Rough broken hills, deep gorges with both sides clothed with a thick growth of quaking ash making a lovely tender green, in startling contrast to the bright yellow of the bunch grass. Foaming streams of water rushing down the gorges, and up and beyond, the dark masses of pines, reaching up to the mountain tops, capped with glistening white snow, and, over and above all, the glorious canopy of the bright blue sky. There is certainly a wonderful brightness of colour in this whole country, when it is flooded, as it usually is, with sunshine; and something exhilarating about it, which defies depression of spirits and makes one feel light-hearted and joyous as a child. It was delicious to jump up at daybreak, with a whole day of delight before us. For it *is* a pleasure to spend a whole day riding over your free grouse moor or deer forest, with the certainty of a good day's sport amongst grouse and prairie chicken, and a possibility of white and black tail deer, bear, or even the monarch of these mountains, the mighty Wapiti itself. There is pleasure too in sitting round the camp-fire in the chilly mornings, warming your hands and cooking breakfast, which you are more than ready for, with the appetite acquired from mountain air and a good conscience. To feel that you are safe for that day, at least, from bad news, or any of the toils and troubles of this work-a-day world. Then, breakfast over, to put a frugal lunch in your pocket, mount your horse and away, to wander at your own sweet will (with no one to say you " nay ") over your vast hunting ground.

When we struck game of any sort, the boys would tumble off their horses, and leave me to catch them as best I could, while they hit or missed, as the case might be. Another time we would picket our horses and go afoot, through bunch-grass knee-high, or make our way as best we could, through the dense groves of brush and quaking ash. Following Jem through one of these, I saw him stop suddenly and beckon to me; there, not two yards in front of him, was an immense rattle-snake, with its head up ready to strike, and rattling with all its might. Such a wicked sound and evil-looking brute. We watched it for some seconds, until Jem put up his gun and blew its head off. It was the first one I had seen, and I never wish to see another. It had ten rattles and was very nearly four feet long. Another step or two, and Jem must have trodden on it, and there would not have been much chance for a man to recover from a bite up there, miles away from any remedies.

Then towards evening we would make our way back to camp, laden with feathered game and a settled conviction that, to-morrow at any rate, we should kill a deer, as we had found plenty of tracks that day. So presently we would get into camp, light the fire, cook supper, and then sit round the blazing logs, pleasantly tired, and chat until some one proposed turning in. There is a wonderful charm about this sort of gipsy life, and it is the most perfect rest.

However, our holiday was cut short, and not in the pleasantest way. I got a kind of sunstroke, and was rather bad all night and the next day; so Jem thought it best to break up our camp and go home. We started early and went right through in one day, reaching home about 11 P.M. We got off the trail in the dark and had to get out and grope with our hands for the ruts. Luckily there were no prickly pears or rattle-snakes about.

We got home on Thursday and the A——'s and Mr. H—— were to come to us on Saturday, to stay until Monday. The amount of dust that had accumulated in our absence was fearful, and I was in despair of ever getting the house cleaned and tidied in time. However, Jem put in a whole day helping me, and by Saturday evening I felt I could receive my guests with an easy conscience. Even out here, you see, a woman can't forget her instincts, and anything like dust and dirt is an abhorrence.

Our guests arrived about 6 o'clock in the even. ing, and, while Jem was helping them to make their horses comfortable, Frank and I were busy in the kitchen ; we had arranged flowers on the table in the morning, and, with a snowy table-cloth and bright silver, I thought our dinner-table looked quite gay. We had a delightful evening and were all very jolly. These little gatherings are very enjoyable to us exiles, and give one a taste of what this country might be, if it was settled more thickly with English people.

Whilst the A——s were with us, we had a sort of tea picnic, which was rather fun. The others had been fishing all day (I have not been able to go out in the sun, since I was ill in the mountains), so, about 5 o'clock, I put Jem's saddle on a very sedate old mare, and sallied out to find them, laden with a basket well stocked with tea, cake, &c. I needn't say my arrival was hailed with acclamation, and we all fell to in high glee. The fish ought to have been grateful to me, as, after tea, the men declared they had caught fish enough (in fact, there was a noble heap of slain on the grass), and voted in favour of sitting under the trees to smoke and chat; so there we sat, talking about "the old countrie" until our duties summoned us home. To-morrow we begin harvest, so there won't be much leisure until it is over.

You ask me about vegetables. This year was not a great success. It's true we had plenty of peas and some spinach and turnips, and we have a grand crop of potatoes; but we did not irrigate enough, so the things got dried up at a critical time and never really recovered from it. Next year we hope to do much better, as we know more about it. I must go and see about my cooking now, so I must close this.

You wonder that I have time to write, when I have so much to do; I confess that it does seem a good deal to do, but it is wonderful how much one can do with a little method; and every day it becomes easier as I get more accustomed to doing everything. It makes one think how little servants must do at home. Here am I, cook, parlour-maid, house-maid, and scullery-maid all rolled into one; and I declare, as long as one's health is good, I would much sooner do it all myself than be bothered with servants; out here, at any rate. In spite of all my work, I have plenty of time to amuse myself, which the American women never seem to do, for they pend their whole time indoors.

August 30th.

SINCE my last letter, I have actually been to a ball! We drove down to Three Forks to stay with the B——'s for the event. They are English people, consisting of a young married couple, her father, sister, and brother; so they make quite an addition to our English society.

To return to the ball. It began about 8 o'clock, and was held in the dining-room of the hotel. I wore my red day dress, as Mrs. B—— told me no one wore evening dresses. When we arrived we found the room full of people, the women dressed up in all sorts of costumes—the belles of the ball, two sisters, in red cotton-backed satin skirts and curtain-muslin tops—and the men, some in black coats, some in brown coats, and some in no coats at all. Such a queer-looking lot!

We had made up our minds only to dance amongst ourselves, and as we were a party of ten or twelve, we could manage very well. The *band* consisted of a fiddle and a banjo, and played the

8

same tune all the way through.   The players sat
on a raised platform, and on the same place stood
a little man, looking full of importance, in dress
clothes and white kid gloves, waving a stick.
He proved to be the Master of the Ceremonies.

"Every man has a number marked on his
ticket, from one to thirty-six, or whatever the
number of men may be.   Only the men pay for
tickets, and invite the ladies."

I soon discovered the reason of the numbered
tickets, for presently the M.C. called out " One,
five, eight, ten," and so on—naming about sixteen numbers—"will dance the next dance.   Get
your partners."

You see there are many more men than
women, so the M.C. calls out who are to dance
so as to give all the men an equal chance of
dancing (liberty, equality, and fraternity!) ; otherwise only a favoured few would get any dancing,
and all the rest would be left out in the cold.
Then the sets were formed, and, to my great
surprise, the M.C. called out what they were to
do in each figure—for instance, " Swing your

partners twice to the right, and return to your places." "Advance and retire twice, swing your partners to the right, and return to your places." Every now and then he uttered a strange yell, which I thought must be an old Indian battle-cry, sounding like "Elemengo," but this, being interpreted, was French (?) "À la main gauche."

Most of the dances were squares, but they had a few waltzes. These were beautifully danced, though very slowly. I never saw better dancing, the only peculiarity being that the man put *both* hands round the girl's waist, clasping them behind, first of all carefully spreading a silk handkerchief on her back to prevent his hands soiling her dress. A most delicate and certainly necessary attention, as the men wore no gloves. The girl put one hand on each of her partner's shoulders. At the end of each dance the M.C. sung out "All promenade." Whereupon they all marched round the room arm-in-arm, generally in solemn silence. In fact, from the absence of conversation and the solemnity of their faces, you might have imagined that they

8 *

were performing a religious ceremony. Do not the English, but also all English-speaking nations, take their pleasure sadly? Certainly these people do, as regards dancing, at any rate.

About 12 o'clock they trooped off to supper. We waited until they were all settled, and then we went down and found a capital supper—chicken, chicken salad, several kinds of cakes, coffee and tea. All this was nicely cooked by a Chinaman. About 1 o'clock the scene began to get rather animated, some of the men beginning actually to talk and even shout. An Englishman whispered to me "Whisky," and advised us to beat a retreat, as, he said, these dances generally degenerated into a bear fight, and frequently a man fight, towards morning; so we quietly departed, rather pleasantly surprised at a ball in the Rockies.

The natives are passionately fond of dancing, and think nothing of driving thirty or forty miles to a ball. They kept this oné up until 7 o'clock in the morning. Girls are certainly favoured out here—not the smallest chance of posing as a wallflower; and in the more important matter of choosing partners for life, it is literally only a case of choice, as the men outnumber the women ten to one. Matrimony, like death, spares neither age nor condition. I have seen young girls of thirteen and hideous old girls of fifty snapped up eagerly as soon as they arrived in the country, which reminds me of the advice given by an old lady to a young wife going out to the Colonies, and looking out for a maid to accompany her. "Take a pretty one, my dear," said the old lady, " for, ugly or pretty, she will have an offer of marriage before she has been out a week ; and while your ugly girl will say ' Yes ' to the first offer she gets and leave you, your pretty one will be harder to please, and will say ' No ' several times before she consents."

Marriages are very simple affairs out here. They are generally performed by a Justice of the Peace, *not* assisted by any representative of any church, and in strict privacy. One couple we know (all this, of course, refers only to natives) were actually married on the open prairie, sitting

in their waggon, while the J. P. sat in his buggy !
A funeral is a much grander affair. All the
neighbours turn out in waggons, buggies, and
saddle-horses, to follow a corpse to the grave, in
a long and melancholy procession. The other
day a deputation waited on Jem to ask if the
Company (of which he is manager, and which
owns most of the land round here) would give a
piece of land for a cemetery.

One of the deputation suggested a certain hill,
because " they would be nice and dry up there."
On Jem saying he would consider the matter,
one man said, " Well, I guess you must be quick,
because old man Morrison's woman is dying;
she can't last more than a week, and he wants to
be sure of a place to put her."

September 6th.

I 'M so delighted to hear that there is a chance of G——coming out here. He might come out here next spring, and stay with us six months, to see if he liked the country and life, and then go home for the winter before settling down here for good. Jem says that is the only thing to do; that it is quite impossible to say whether anyone will like the life and get on, or to say what they had better do. He says he thinks there are plenty of good openings here, but everything depends upon the man himself.

Of course G——could not do any hard work, and there would be no occasion for him to do any. No one does except "grangers," for I don't call riding after stock "hard work." Of course it is, really, but still it is very different to the regular manual "grind" of a farm-hand. I don't think *gentlemen* are fitted for that. Jem and Frank have tried it this summer, just to show they could do it at a pinch, but it has nearly killed them, working so hard at things they are not accustomed to in this frightful heat. They both say they will never try it again.

I think gentlemen are inclined to work too hard for the first few hours, and are then utterly exhausted and dead for the remainder of the day, and yet feel obliged to go on to the end. They can't work steadily and quietly like a working man who has been used to it all his life. It is just like putting a high-mettled, well-bred horse to plough with a cold-blooded cart-horse. The thoroughbred wears himself out by trying to do too much at first, whereas the cart-horse goes steadily lugging all day without exciting himself. Jem says that he thinks an Englishman, who has been used to hunting in England and ridden all his life, can kill a Western American when it comes to riding, and that he can ride greater distances with greater ease to himself and the horse he is on; and that stock-work is all that an Englishman is good for, if he wants to go in for hard work, though, of course,

it is useful for him to know how to do all kinds
of ordinary farm-work.

They call the farmers here "grangers," as
distinct from ranch-men or stock-men, and it is
rather a term of reproach—not quite that, either
—but still the granger is held in low estimation
by the stock-man. In Montana the latter is
king, and all the laws seem framed to his advantage and to the disadvantage of the granger.

The term "ranche" really means the same as
the English word "farm." I used to think that
a ranche consisted of thousands of acres, like
the Australian "run"; but now I find that a
little farm of even forty acres, with a one-roomed
log cabin, is a "ranche," and what we call the
"range" answers to the Australian "run," with
this difference, that whereas the Australian pays
rent for or owns his "run," and has it all to
himself, fenced in, the Western stock-man has
his range free, but his stock run in common
with several other peoples', and are not fenced in
except by the natural boundaries of the range,
such as rivers or chains of mountains. Thus

our range extends over some three or four
hundred thousand acres, and is bounded on
three sides by rivers and one side by a chain of
high mountains.

The cowboy on his hardy pony is the Western
rancher's wire fence, and it is his duty to see
that no stock strays outside the natural boundaries of the range, and to bring back any that
do. There are lots of our horses which we don't
see more than once a year, but we don't feel
uneasy about them, as if they should stray off
the range we should probably hear of them. Of
course stock-men lose some by straying every
year, but the loss sustained is a very small rent
to pay for the enormous amount of land on which
the stock run.

If G—— comes out here only for his health, he
could not come to a better country. People
from the Eastern States, suffering from chest
complaints, come here and get quite well and
strong. The Morrises were an example of this.
Their horrid coughs got less and less all last winter,
even in the very cold weather, and finally

vanished altogether. They said they were never free from a cough in England. Then G—— could ride, shoot, and fish to his heart's content. I have been fishing every day this week, and kept the larder well supplied, as the boys have been too busy harvesting to have time for shooting or fishing. Jem gave me a new fishing rod.

I was out on the range hunting horses yesterday, found what I wanted, and drove them in all by myself, feeling very proud of my performance. Jem says I shall soon make a first-rate cowboy. I tried my hand with the lasso one day and caught a little colt, as he ran by, at the first attempt, but would not spoil it by trying again; so I looked very grand and said "I wondered that men ever missed, and that I knew it was quite easy, though they did make such a fuss about it."

Frank has just been out shooting, as the rain stopped their work, and brought in any amount of teal and duck, enough to last a week. I have learnt to salt fish, so that they will keep good for a week or ten days. We are all going down to stay with Mr. H—— for two nights next week. Mr. H—— and Harry were staying with us this week.

September 20th.

Such a letter from a dear friend in England this week! "How can I do such dreadful things? Camping out amongst rattle-snakes! getting sunstrokes! driving wild horses! and, as if these out-of-door terrors weren't bad enough, working like a slave indoors and killing myself with hard work."

Does it sound so appalling? Well, it never struck me as being anything out of the way at the time. But, of course, things out here *appear* worse to people at home than they really are.

Now for the reverse side of the medal. I pass over the rattle-snakes. Sunstroke—now you might get that in England—and, then, I only mentioned it to show how hot it is, for you know I always rather boasted of being able to stand extremes of heat and cold. Driving wild horses! Well, perhaps that *sounds* appalling; but it doesn't mean driving them in harness, but riding another horse behind them and driving them, like you see an old man driving up the milk cows at home, only the old man is on foot and the cows don't go out of a walk.

Now for the other indictment—Indoors. Now I like the work. When you have no society, and everyone is *out of doors* working, you *must* work for amusement *indoors*. I do think this is the best sort of life. One feels so much better and happier; and so would any other healthy girl. Of course, washing dishes, scrubbing floors, and all the rest of it, does sound and seem a great hardship to people at home; but I can assure you it doesn't seem so when you do it. I know I would not exchange my happy, free, busy,

healthy life out here, for the weariness and
ennui that makes so many girls at home miserable.
I don't feel myself to be an object of pity—quite
the reverse ; I only wonder that more people who
are miserable on small incomes at home, don't
come out here and be happy. What is poverty
at home would be riches out here, and one
doesn't have to spend half one's income in
keeping up appearances ; and there 's the glorious
health everyone enjoys in this country. How
many thousands a year is that worth ?

No ! I think people out here, with moderate
means, are infinitely happier than people in the
same condition at home. What do you gain by
being out here ? Health and happiness, plenty
to do, plenty of interests and amusements. Indoors you can have your piano, all the newest
books at a fraction of the price you have to pay
at home (I am reading the latest three-volume
novel, which costs a guinea at home, and costs me
a shilling here), all the periodicals and English
papers—a little late, perhaps, but what does that
matter ?—and you can see a fellow-mortal now

and then to discuss them all with. Out of doors
you have your horses, your grouse-moor, deer-
forests, and all free. Let us see what you lose.
Society, and the luxury of sitting with your
hands folded, seeing others do badly what you
feel you can do much better yourself. As a
drawback even to this latter luxury, you have the
endless bother of servants, and as for Society,
we shall get that by degrees. You will say,
" All very well while you 're young." Granted ;
and when we are old it will be time enough
" to creep home, and take our place there,
the sick and old among." Meanwhile I am
thoroughly happy with my varied occupations
and amusements, and if I have some cares (and
who has not ?), have I not many joys to counter-
balance them ; so give me my home in

> The West, the West, the land of the free,
> Where the mighty Missouri rolls down to the sea,

and I am more than content.

September 26th.

LAST week I spent two or three days with the
B——s, and left Jem alone in his glory, as Frank
was away. Having cooked enough to last until
I came back, I put on a clean frock, climbed up
into the buggy, and drove off, enjoying my drive
immensely.

Perhaps I shouldn't have enjoyed it quite so
much, if I had known that the Helena coach was
stopped the other day by highwaymen, or "road
agents," as they are called. No one was hurt,
however, or robbed, as one of the "road agents"
had warned the proprietors, and agreed to help
to capture his accomplice when the attempt was
made, which he did successfully; and this
Western Dick Turpin is now cooling his heels in
jail. Highway robbers, or "road agents," are
scarce now, though some years ago they were as
plentiful as blackberries. I heard such a capital
story of the presence of mind of a lady on one

occasion, when a coach was stopped, that I must tell it to you.

She was travelling by coach (before the days of railroads) to join her husband, a distance of some hundred miles. On the journey one of her fellow-passengers said to her :

"I have got about a thousand dollars in my pocket-book, and feel rather uneasy about road agents. Would you mind concealing it in your dress, and giving it to me at the end of the journey? If we are stopped, they are less likely to search you than me."

She complied with his request, and accordingly hid the money in her dress. Towards evening there was a shout of "Throw up your hands!" and four men on horseback, with masked faces, appeared in the road, pointing their pistols at the driver, who promptly pulled up.

Two men then appeared at the side of the coach, and ordered the passengers to give up their arms, which they did. The robbers then ordered them to "shell out." Our friend of the morning gave up a few dollars, and was con-

9

gratulating himself on the success of his pre-
caution, when, to his horror, the lady said in a
clear voice:

"I have got a thousand dollars, but I suppose
I must give them up," producing at the same
time our friend's hardly-earned roll of "green-
backs" from the folds of her dress.

He looked unutterable things. The robbers
then rifled the treasure-box, and rode off delighted
with their booty.

As soon as they were gone, our friend began
abusing the lady in no measured terms, accusing
her of having betrayed him, and given up all he
had in the world, out of sheer fright. She only
replied oracularly that "he would see," and that
she could give no explanation now.

When she got to the end of her journey, she
asked him to come and stay the night at her
house, adding that her husband would be very
glad to see him. To this he assented, saying, in
an injured tone of voice, that it was the least
she could do, seeing that through her treachery
he was without a cent in the world. He wsa

royally entertained, his hostess exerting herself
to amuse him; but not a word of explanation
was vouchsafed by either host or hostess, and he
went to bed in no very enviable state of mind.

On entering the dining-room in the morning,
he was met by his host, who said :

" Here are your thousand dollars, which my
wife ventured to borrow in a case of emergency.
The fact was she had twenty thousand dollars,
which she was bringing to me, concealed in her
dress, and she thought that by giving up at once
the thousand dollars entrusted to her by you she
would disarm suspicion, and save any further
search on the part of the robbers. Her quickness, as you know now, saved me from a heavy
loss."

Our friend apologized for his unfounded suspi-
cions and rudeness of the previous day; and
breakfast, no doubt, proved a far cheerier meal
than the supper of the night before.

I spent two days with the B——'s and enjoyed
myself very much. They have got a piano, and
are all musical; some young Englishmen came to

9 *

supper one night, who all sang very well; so we had plenty of singing, and, as a wind up, a miniature dance. I say "miniature," because the room was only large enough for one couple at a time; I brought Mrs. B—— home with me to stay a few days, to have a little rest, which she much needed. She stayed with us about a week, and, when my work was done, I drove her about in the buggy: we went some most beautiful drives, either up in the mountains or down by the river.

The autumn tints are beginning, the cotton-wood leaves turn such gorgeous yellows and reds, and, mixed with the green of the cedar, the colourings are perfectly grand.

Yesterday Jem and I drove to Bozeman to do some shopping; started at half-past seven, crossed one river and several creeks, and got into town at half-past eleven. It was eighteen miles of an abominable road full of great round stones; the smallest as big as a cricket-ball and some a good deal bigger than a man's head, and then, when we got within five miles of Bozeman, and amongst the settlements, we got into lanes, *i.e.*

where the road is fenced on both sides. Here the soil was a rich black loam, and very wet, and the road fearfully cut up by waggon-wheels; so our wheels were nearly up to the axles in ruts. We got a capital luncheon at a small hotel and then went shopping.

It was quite nice to wear a decent frock again and drive a good-looking pair of horses through a town. The worst of it was, our horses would not stand, so the people had to take a running shot at the buggy with their parcels. It amuses me the way we have to shake hands and say "How do you do" to all our shopkeepers, before any business can be done. Our drive home was very enjoyable, and we got back about 7 o'clock.

We have been storing our potato crop, about 200 bushels off half an acre. Potatoes, and in fact everything which we don't want to have frozen, have to be stored in an underground cellar, at a depth of about eight feet. They dig a hole in the ground about eight feet deep, eight to ten feet long, and seven to eight feet wide. They then make a door-way with steps going down into the hole and roof it all over, piling up the earth taken out to a height of four feet. The first houses in this country were made in the same way and called " dug-outs."

———

October 10th.

Mrs. B—— left us two or three days ago, to my great regret. It was so nice having someone to gossip to all the time I was working. She had rather a nasty accident on the way home. Her sister drove over from Three Forks to fetch her, lunched here, and, about 2.30, they started to go home.

It was bitterly cold. When they were about three miles from home, they came to a place where the road forked, both roads going to the same place, but one rather shorter than the other.

They took the shortest road, though it was not
the one by which Miss M—— had come in
the morning. This brought them to a creek; the
usual crossing, where the water is wide and
shallow, was frozen solid, and the ice like glass.
The horses would not face it, so Mrs. B—— tried
to cross a little lower down at a narrow place,
where the water was not frozen. The horses did
not like this much better, at last one of them
made a jump and the other held back. One never
knows exactly how these things happen, but Miss
M—— was thrown out of the buggy, clean on to
the bank; when she picked herself up, she saw
Mrs. B—— and the horses all struggling together
in the water. She contrived to extract her sister;
but, do what they would, they could not get the
horses out.

Meanwhile Mrs. B——'s clothes were frozen as
stiff as a board. So Miss M—— pulled off her
own dry shoes and stockings, and made Mrs.
B—— exchange her wet ones for these dry ones.
She then took off her own wraps and piled them
on to Mrs. B——, and started off to walk bare-

footed, over gravel, sage brush, and prickly pear, to the nearest house for assistance. The owner, an American, refused to turn out; so there was nothing to be done, but to go back and bring Mrs. B—— to the house, where the woman kindly supplied her with dry clothes.

Miss M—— then walked home, and Mr. B—— drove to the scene of the accident as hard as he could go. The horses and buggy were got out of the creek; curiously enough, no damage had been done. They all drove home, and, we hear, none of the party are any the worse for the accident.

I've taken to cooking more now that the hot weather is gone, and invent all kinds of little puddings in a very simple way. They are considered wonderful productions, though, by the boys. That is one great thing in this country. Everything you cook is voted good, because everybody is well, and everybody is hungry. I potted a whole heap of eggs in dry salt in the summer, and have not found a bad one yet.

October 12th.

I AM afraid you will think my last letter rather short, but I met with a nasty accident, which laid me up for some days, and I can only hobble about now. I was riding on the range with Jem, when the horse I was riding suddenly pitched on his head, and rolled on to my foot. When he got up, my foot was caught fast in the stirrup, but, by the greatest good luck, Frank had oiled the patent safety arrangement only the day before, so it acted all right, and my foot got free. If I had had an ordinary stirrup, or the patent safety arrangement had not been in working order, I must have been killed, as my mount was a young " scarey " horse and would have dragged me for miles. As it was Jem had a hard job to catch him. When I got up, I found that I could not put my foot to the ground, and that it was giving me excruciating pain. What was to be done? Here we were, eight miles from the nearest house, and it seemed impossible to ride in such pain. However, as I refused to be left alone until Jem could go and fetch a conveyance, there was nothing for it but to mount as best I could, and ride to the nearest house. I would rather not have that ride over again !

The women at the ranche took me in hand, and were very kind. They thought there were no bones broken, and strongly advised Jem *not* to send for the doctor, as doctors, in their opinion, were not likely to do any good, but were quite certain to send in a long bill. Jem went home for the buggy, came back, and drove me home.

I was in great pain all night, so we telegraphed for the doctor, who came in the afternoon from Bozeman. He seemed a very nice, clever man. He found that two toes were dislocated, but was not sure about the ankle; he put the toes in, which was a very painful operation, and then told me that I had better have ether while he examined the ankle, as he could then make a more thorough examination ; so I had ether, and he found that the ankle was not actually dislocated, though very badly sprained. The doctor's fee was five guineas, which does not seem very outrageous for this country, as he had come eighteen miles, and could not get back that night.

I am having a nice rest now, as the boys do everything and make most amusing nurses. Frank is cook and Jem house-maid, &c. He *thinks* he is first-rate in the latter department, but I'm afraid there will be a great accumulation of dust when I get back to my duties again.

December 8th.

I THINK by the time you get this it will be Christmas. How quickly the year does seem to have gone! Next year I hope we may all be together in the old country.

Last year at this time we had deep snow and
the thermometer down to 50 below zero. This
year we have had no snow at all down here, and
the other day a chinook cleared even the mountains. The weather is simply perfect, the sun
shining all day, and still quite warm. Everyone
says that the climate is getting less severe, and I
suppose the more the country gets settled the
milder the winters will become. At least, that
seems to have been the case in other Western
States, so I don't see why Montana should not
follow suit. All stock is looking fat and well;
people have not had to feed even their dairy
stock. However, some of our thoroughbred
mares don't seem to agree with this arrangement, for a whole lot of them came trooping
home from the range of their own accord the
other day, and now stand round the house and
stables every morning, looking sulky and evidently expecting to be fed.

We drove to Three Forks the other day in an
hour and twenty minutes. Jem calls it fourteen
miles, so I think we made good time.

All the English people down there were in ecstasies over the result of the elections at home. Somehow or other all the Englishmen out here seem to be staunch Conservatives, which is a great loss to the party at home.

Mr. H—— and three others have just returned from a month's hunt. They brought back about a ton of venison, which they have been distributing amongst their friends. We came in for a haunch of elk, which proved excellent, such nice tender meat. One of the party shot an enormous bull elk which fell down a precipice, so he had to content himself with only getting the hide and the head. The antlers were magnificent. Altogether the party were highly delighted with their month's sport, as they got bear, elk, and two or three kinds of deer, and had a very jolly time into the bargain, as there were five other Englishmen hunting in the district. They all camped together and, as you may imagine, had jolly nights round the camp-fire.

I have asked four Englishmen to come and dine and sleep on Christmas day, so we shall be a large party. They all bring their own blankets and sleep on the floor, as there is only one spare bed between them. They are to bring the turkey and we are going to kill a steer, which will provide the traditional sirloin and the suet for the pudding. It is rather an amusing way of giving a dinner for your guests to bring part of the provisions. As one winter is much the same as another out here, the description of our doings last winter will suffice for this.

February 20th.

THE winter is nearly over now, we hope, so I am going to tell you a little about my experiences of a winter out here without servants. The worst part of it certainly is the getting up in the morning to light the fires; the house is so fearfully cold. One morning the thermometer in our drawing-room registered ten below zero, which

is as low as it goes. The bread was frozen solid,
and took an hour to thaw out before we could
have breakfast. There is a stove in our bed-
room, which Jem gets ready over night. First
he cuts a lot of shavings, which are laid at the
bottom of the stove, and on the top of these a
lot of dry wood; then the whole is sprinkled
with paraffin oil and ready to catch fire in a
moment.

About 7 o'clock in the morning Jem jumps
up, lights the stove, and goes to bed again. In
twenty minutes our room is as warm as possible;
then we get up and dress. Jem used to light
the kitchen fire, which is also laid over-night, on
his way to the stables, but as he was not very
successful in getting it to burn, I do it myself
now. While he is feeding the horses, I get
breakfast ready and light the fire in the dining-
room. By the time breakfast is ready the rooms
are warm. Stoves are certainly less trouble than
fire-places, consume less wood, and warm a room
very quickly. In the dining-room there is an
'Angela" stove, which is very pretty, having a

transparent front, so that you can see the fire or you can open the door in front, and then it is almost as good as an open fire-place. All this winter I have been out every day and feel tremendously well; in fact, I thoroughly enjoy the dry cold, though the boys rather grumble at it.

Jem says, " It's all very fine, but it's no joke when the handles of the hay-forks burn your hands, unless you have gloves on, and you have to thaw a bit before you can put it in a horse's mouth, to prevent it sticking to his tongue."

A young Englishman, during his first winter out here, doubted the latter fact, and experimented on his own tongue. The result was that when he felt the frozen steel burn, he snatched it away, and a small piece of his tongue came with it. The sceptic was converted. We either thaw the bits out in the oven, or dip them in water, before bridling a horse, which prevents them sticking.

A horse's life out here during the winter in a stable can hardly be a happy one. The stables are desperately cold, being built of wood, often only a single half-inch plank. Ours are built of double boards, with a space of eight inches stuffed with straw between the boards; and yet, in the morning, in very cold weather, icicles hang from the horses' noses and eye-lids, and their bodies are white with frost! In spite of this they do very well; even imported horses have wintered out here their first winter in sheds full of holes, and half the roof off, and have been none the worse for it.

It seems to me that horses don't mind *dry* cold in the least. I think if I was a Montana horse, I should prefer wintering out of doors to being in a stable. If they are out of doors they can move about to keep warm, and the very fact of having to paw for their food must help to keep up the circulation; but imagine being tied up and unable to move, in one of these desperately cold stables.

Jem has been amusing himself with bitting our two-year olds, saddling them up, and putting harness on them. He gets so interested that he

10

forgets all about the cold, and will sit for an hour at a time, pipe in mouth, lost in admiration of some colt, which promises to carry himself in good form. Then, of course, I have to come out to help to admire, and sometimes to put on or to take off the tackle.

We generally tie up one front foot, when we begin breaking a colt, then he can't kick or strike, or get away from you; besides you can jump on his back, and he can't buck. You can do more with a colt in half an hour with his leg tied up, than you can in a week without it. As soon as they find they are in your power, they give up, and when they find you don't hurt them, they soon get gentle.

We have got any amount of little pigs running about—over fifty, and all white. They were born in the brush in the very coldest weather, forty below zero, and with five inches of snow on the ground. Most of them got their ears and tails frozen off, which gives them rather a grotesque appearance. The sows disappeared for a week, and never came near the house. What they lived on all that time I can't imagine. One old lady gobbled up a dead skunk, and made the whole place redolent for some days. I should have thought that no living animal would have eaten skunk; not even the man who said " he *could* eat turkey-buzzard, but didn't *hanker* after it."

It was a great joke getting these little pigs up to the house. About a week after a litter was born, the mother would come up to the house for something to eat. Then Jem would take a sack and follow her tracks, until he came to where the children were. I had to keep the old lady occupied by feeding her, while Jem caught the little ones and put them in the sack. He said it was very hard to catch them, as they would run out of the nest, and get buried in the snow, or hide under some bush or stump. Then he had to put them in a sack, and run like mischief to put them in a warm sty, sometimes pursued by the old sow. These old sows are awfully fierce, and will attack a man in a minute.

10 *

February 25th.

FRANK left us last week, to our very great regret, and now Jem has got a young Englishman, a very nice boy, to help him for a time. They are very busy breaking the yearlings to lead. I enjoy looking on, perched up on the top rail of the corral, and watching them lasso the little things, put the halters on, and then go through a regular tug-of-war performance. They pull the colts about for a few minutes, just to show them what is wanted, and then tie them up all night, and let them teach themselves. In the morning the pupils have learnt their lesson, and will lead anywhere.

The weather is deliciously warm, and people all going about in their shirt-sleeves. Our young Englishman is a capital shot, and keen fisherman, so he keeps us well supplied with game and fish. Jem went off the other day to look at some stock about a hundred miles from here, so I

drove him down to Three Forks, where he hired
a buggy and team, and went on. We started
from here before the sun was up, and, as we drove
along, the sunrise was most beautiful; such wonderful colours on the foot-hills and mountains.
The main range of the Rockies was all covered
with snow, sparkling and glistening in the sun;
the lower range tinted with a lovely rose-colour,
and the range below that a deep purple. Altogether the drive was very enjoyable. We arrived
at Three Forks just as the B——s were finishing
breakfast, so I stayed with them all day, and
drove home in the evening.

One of the bridges which I had to cross had
been damaged by the ice rising, when the latter
broke up, as it always does in the spring. They
had been "fixing" this bridge all day, but hadn't
finished it. One man had been left to look after
it, and there he sat, calmly chewing tobacco, and
whittling a stick—a Western man's sole amusement. I really think they are the best loafers
under the sun. I called out to him to know
what to do, upon which he said: "I guess you'll

have to unhitch." So he helped me to unhitch, and I led the horses, while he dragged the buggy across. We hitched up the horses again on the other side, holding an amicable conversation during the process, in the course of which he told me "he guessed I was pretty well used to horses," at which I felt flattered. I got home safely, and found the young Englishman ready to take the horses, and also that he had got dinner ready, being a very good cook. It seemed quite grand, as if one was at home with a full staff of servants.

Jem got home last night, having driven seventy miles that day, not bad travelling, and he said his horses were not over-tired either. These Western horses can do enormous distances in a day, and day after day without knocking up. Jem rode one fourteen-hand pony eighty-five miles between sunrise and sunset; and the same pony 450 miles in ten days. with fourteen stone on his back, and nothing to eat, except what grass he could get at the end of a picket rope.

We are to have an old man, an American, to look after the horses (and to take care of me !)

as Jem is going to Dakota soon with a batch of
horses.

March 7th.

HERE I am alone in my glory, with no one
to look after me except old Van Vranken, the
American, who is taking care of things while
Jem is away.

A large bunch of horses arrived some days ago,
and we have been very busy getting them ready
for the Dakota market. Old Van is a capital
hand at breaking horses, and we have been driving
all day, sometimes Van and Jem, and sometimes
I, go with one or other of them. About three
inches of snow fell, so we were able to use bob
sleighs. That is certainly a delightful way of

getting over the ground, though these young horses, with nothing to steady them, are apt to go rather faster than one intends; however, as they say out here, "We can ride as fast as they can run." And with the whole prairie to run over, it does not much matter where they go.

Jem nearly always gets me to drive, as he declares I have better hands for driving than he has, so I've had a most exciting time altogether. The day before the horses were shipped—which is a phrase here for sending things by train—two or three men came down to help, and the horses were all thrown, their tails plaited and sewn up in sacking to prevent them gnawing one another's tails or rubbing their own against the side of the truck. The poor things are only taken out of the truck and fed once in twenty-four hours, so you may imagine they are ready to eat horse-hair or anything else.

Some of them were such good-looking horses, that I was quite sorry to see them go. They stood from 15·2 to 16 hands, and I should not have been ashamed to drive some of them in

England. The others were more of the omnibus stamp.

I live by myself in one part of the house and Van by himself in another part. It is rather eerie at night. Being all alone, one notices all sorts of noises, that never bothered one before. The noise the rats make, the hooting of the owls, the howling of the coyotes, even the squealing of the pigs, all make one feel rather jumpy. Of course I know I am in no danger, and old Van, though he is seventy-six years old, is a protection against tramps or anything of that sort, but still I don't quite like being alone. Old Van is a very amusing fellow, and looks on me as his granddaughter, I think.

The other day I was going down to Three Forks, to call on a newly-married English couple —or rather semi-English, for she's an American —and when I was quite ready, came out to the stables in a decent frock. Van seemed immensely struck with this, and stood gazing for a full minute ; then, with a chuckle, said, " Well, we *are* fine." I daresay he was surprised at the transformation scene, as my ordinary get-up is all holes and patches. I am always burning holes in my skirts from going too near the stoves.

The people on whom I went to call seemed very nice, but she declares she can't live at Three Forks; so, after furnishing and fitting up a house there, he will have to leave and go to Helena. She was asking Mrs. B—— all about house-keeping and how ladies manage out here. When Mrs. B—— had finished, she said, "I hope *I* shall never come down to scrubbing *my* floors and cleaning *my* stoves." Mrs. B—— piled it on after that.

Our pigs are increasing rapidly. There are about ninety now, all ages and sizes, running about. Van grumbles, as they make such a mess round the stables, and says "the ground is *paved* with pigs." And it certainly does look like it, when they are lying together in the sun. Thank goodness they don't bother me, as I always greet them with boiling water when they come round the kitchen door.

April 5th.

JEM came back a day or two ago. When he arrived I was staying at Three Forks, and as he did not come back until eleven o'clock at night, the house was all locked up, and he had to get in through the window. He was rather afraid that old Van would mistake him for a burglar or horse-thief, and pepper him with his shot gun, which he always keeps loaded with buck-shot in case of emergency.

I have had two men down here fencing in about twenty acres of brush and rough pasture for the pigs. They fenced it with a stake and bound fence, and we hope to keep the pigs in there until the autumn, and then turn them on to the peas to fatten. One of the men who is working at the fence, plays the violin very well; it is quite a treat to hear him. The men sleep in a tent and have their meals with old Van.

Little colts are coming pretty fast now. I

ride slowly round the pastures every day, and take great interest in the new arrivals. It is so deliciously warm that my horse and I nearly go to sleep, and then I rouse him and myself up by jumping all the fences available.

We are all very much interested in the Home Rule question out here, but no argument is possible, as we are Conservatives to a man. The Americans are all in favour of Home Rule; but it is no use arguing with them, as they don't really understand anything at all about it. How I *should* like to be at home now and get all the news fresh. Of course we get all important news almost as soon as you do, but one misses all the items that lead up to a great event.

Jem talks of driving 300 head of horses back to the States, selling as he goes, until they are all sold. If he does, I shall come home, as I could not stay here for three or four months all alone. Sometimes I have a wild idea of going with him. It would be rather an adventure following the tails of 300 horses 1,500 miles, camping out every night, and shooting and fishing *en route.* They say that after the first fortnight the horses are no trouble at all, that the waggon carrying the tent, provisions, blankets, &c., goes first, and the horses all string out and follow it along the trail, with one or two men behind to keep them going. However, I'm afraid it would not really do for me to go, especially as I heard that some man in Texas, who took his wife and daughter with him on a long cattle-drive, had a difference with his "boys" on account of not letting them eat with his women-folk, whereupon they all left him; and there he was, 100 miles from anywhere, with 2,000 head of cattle and no one to handle them but himself, wife, and daughter. How he got out of the mess I never heard.

May 3rd.

SUCH a lovely day, quite hot and summery. I have just finished my house-work; it is now nearly 1 P.M., and I have been terribly busy since 6 o'clock this morning. Jem starts directly after breakfast every morning now, as he is riding on the horse round-up, and I don't see him again all day. I am going to ride with him to-morrow, which will be great fun. No sooner had he started this morning than Van comes to me, and, in a coaxing tone of voice, persuades me to jump on my horse and drive in a bunch of mares for him. I had such a nice ride round after them, and helped a man, whom I didn't know, to drive some cows, which he had found near our place, part of the way home. Then I drove our mares in, unsaddled my horse, and went and toiled at what Jem calls my " Fetish," *i.e.* house-cleaning.

I always clean out the drawing-room and bed-room on Mondays, filling up the hall with furniture, like the maids do at home. I think I do it in a very scientific way, and if I dust a single thing out of its turn, it quite puts me out. Just as I had got all the things nicely placed in the hall and could hardly open the front door, an Englishman living near us must needs come and call; so I invited him in, but told him he would have to sit on the floor. He promised, instead, to come back when I had finished.

I must tell you what a splendid plan I have found for scrubbing the kitchen floor. No more going down on my hands and knees and scrubbing with a brush. Now I do it with a mop —made out of an old broom-handle and one of Jem's old flannel shirts—and a bucket of boiling water with some lye in it. This I mop about the floor, and dry it all up with a clean cloth. Lye is wonderful stuff, and makes the boards as white as snow. I was so delighted last Saturday when I found out what a success my new plan was, as scrubbing that floor used to weigh on my mind nearly all the week.

We expect Harry L—— out this week from England, and then I shall get my nice, cool summer dresses. I find holland in summer, and heavy thick serge in winter, are the best stuffs to wear out here.

Now the sun has gone down a bit, I am going to saddle up and go on a private round-up on my own account. I have just been up on the hill, and have seen hundreds of horses being driven into the corral at the Horse Ranche; so I expect Jem will be coming down here soon with a bunch of ours, and will want me to help him. I am afraid I shall only be able to ride this summer either very early or very late, as even yesterday I found the sun rather too much for my head, and I don't want to be affected by it again, as I was last summer.

I forget whether I told you all about the round-up before. On a fixed day all the people who own horses on the range meet at a certain place, and all ride off together into the hills. Then, when they have gone some miles, the captain of the round-up tells them to spread out into a wide half-circle and ride towards home, driving in all the horses which they see. Presently the hills seem to be alive with horses, all galloping in the same direction, with their manes and tails flying in the wind, and the men all galloping after them up and down hills and ravines, over badger-holes and small dry watercourses. Now and then, though not often, as the horses are so wonderfully clever over rough ground, you see a man and horse turn a complete somersault, the horse having put his fore-feet into a badger-hole; but this is only treated as a joke, and the fallen generally pick themselves up none the worse, and are at it again. Sometimes a band of horses strike back for the hills, which treats you to a glorious gallop to head them off. Altogether it is most exciting. As they get near the corral the separate bunches become merged into one huge band, and you can see nothing but hundreds of horses galloping, and clouds of dust. Then two or three men on the fastest horses gallop on ahead, let down the bars of the corral, and stand in front of the horses to turn them in.

11

On they come, until they are headed by these
men. Then they begin huddling together, circling round, getting their heads turned the wrong
way, and acting generally in the most provoking
manner possible. " Bronchos " seem to have the
greatest objection to going into a corral.

Very often an old gentle horse, who no more
minds going into the corral than into his own
stable, stands just in the gateway, blocking it up,
and looking as if he was frightened to death at
going in; till you long to be near him with a
good thick stick. At last a few make up their
minds to go in. The rest follow pell-mell like
a flock of sheep; the bars are put up, saddle-
horses led away reeking with sweat, and tied up to
a post, with a forty-pound saddle on their backs
to rest (?) ; and cutting out, which I have told you
about before, begins.

When this is all over, the " boys " indulge in a
little fun. Some one or other has got a four-year-
old "broncho" which he wants ridden; accordingly some enterprising individual offers to ride
him, if the " boys " will make up a purse to see

the fun. So the hat goes round, and is soon returned with a contribution of eight or nine dollars; not bad pay for riding a "broncho" once. Half a dozen lassoes are soon whirling in the air; the luckless "broncho" is caught by the forelegs, and comes down with a thud that might be heard a hundred yards away; someone jumps on his head, a bit is forced into his mouth, and, for the first time in his life, he finds himself bridled. A handkerchief is then fastened over his eyes to blindfold him, and he receives a hearty kick in the ribs, or someone jumps with both feet on his side, as a friendly (?) intimation to get up. As soon as he is on his legs, a heavy Mexican saddle is clapped on to his back, and the girths drawn as tight as possible. Then he is hauled outside the corral with a running accompaniment of kicks and blows. The "broncho" rider climbs gingerly into the saddle, leans forward to pull off the handkerchief, then settles himself well back in the saddle, and, if the broncho does not start at once, plunges the heavy Mexican spurs into the unfortunate animal's shoulders, and away they go; the quadruped

11 *

bucking and bawling, or running for dear life, and the biped whooping, yelling, flogging, and spurring to his heart's content. A rough school, and no wonder that the young idea takes to buck-jumping as naturally as a duck to water.

July 10th.

I THINK by this time my letters will have given you a fair idea of a lady's life in the Far West, with its daily routine.

Now I am going to give you a resumé of this summer, and then I shall have brought a history of nearly two years to a close. To begin with, I have been alone nearly the whole summer. After the horse round-up, Jem was away all the time shipping horses, except for one or two days, at intervals of three or four weeks; so there I was with old Van, the horses, and the pigs. But you must not imagine that the time hung heavily on my hands. On the contrary, I was busy from morning to night. Lonely I was, of course, as sometimes I did not see a soul except Van, who was always very good, for days at a time. When I say Van was good, I mean he was nice to me; otherwise I had to do what he ought to have done, for he was old and very loth to get on a horse, so I did all the riding.

Every morning at ten o'clock I used to turn the whole band of horses, which we keep on our own ranche, outside the gates to graze; then at one o'clock I rode about three or four miles to see that they were not straying off back to the hills; then again at night I rounded them all up and brought them home. The pigs also were no small source of annoyance, for they were always getting out, and into mischief. So I had to spend half my time chasing them home again. I used to carry them several buckets full of potatoes every day, and feed them inside the fence, by way of keeping them contented. You would have laughed to see me, leaning over the pig-fence, with a bucketful of potatoes in my hand, uttering unearthly yells of " Piggy, pig, piggy ! " to call them to the feast. Besides this, I used to ride round the fences every night to see that they were all right; so you may imagine that, with all this and the house, I had enough to do.

The evenings were the worst part of it. It was so fearfully lonely, sitting all by oneself. Of course I had my piano, and Jem sent me books every week, and there were the English papers, but still these are not company; even my dog " Rook " and black cat " Jack " seemed more satisfactory in that respect. About once a week some of the Englishmen would come to call, and I made the acquaintance of a "granger's" wife, whom I visited nearly every day to get milk (as our cow is dry); but, of course, this did not lessen the loneliness of my evenings. I don't think I could stand another summer alone, it is so trying to one's nerves.

I had eventually to sell all the pigs, as it was impossible to keep them in; so I rode about trying to find customers for them, and a hard job it was, for, of course, no one wants to buy pigs in the middle of summer. However, I triumphed at last, and got rid of them all at some price or another. It was a great satisfaction when I saw the last batch go off in the waggon. I managed better with my horses, as I was able to keep them together, and I must say I love that work; it is so interesting to watch the little colts growing, and I know every animal in the herd. In the evenings I often used to take a panful of salt, and get the whole band round me; even the shyest in the whole band eventually came up to me to get its share.

Our big black horse was taken very ill with pneumonia, and I was dreadfully anxious about him. He was so weak one day that I thought he must die; so I told Van that the horse wanted stimulants, and nothing else would save him. Van said he didn't know what to do, he daren't leave the horse, and there were no stimulants in the house; so I saddled up Sinister, my cow-pony, and galloped up to town, went straight to

the saloon, and asked for a bottle of whisky. I
don't know what the bar-keeper thought. The
horse began to mend as soon as he had the
whisky, and eventually got well. But when our
bill came in from the " store," we four l a bottle
of whisky charged against us every day for a
month! We never knew how much of it the
horse got! If he got it all, I am surprised that
he is alive; for they say this Western whisky is
fearful stuff, in fact, the natives call it, " Kill at
forty rods ! "

Jem came home on my birthday, and said that
I must go back to England at once, for he should
have to be away on and off until November, and
I must not be left alone here any longer ; so I am
really coming home. Jem is going to move all
our best horses to a new range, about eleven
miles from here, and put a man in charge. We
have let this ranche to two Englishmen, and
arranged everything, so that I can go home at
once, and Jem will follow in December.

Of course, I am fearfully busy, packing up all
my household gods, and getting ready to start,

and awfully excited about coming home.
be sorry to leave this country, and the ranche, and
all my pets; but, of course, it will be delicious
to see everybody at home again, and I am very
curious to see how I shall like the old life after
a long absence from it.

February 20th.

Here I am back in England again. The journey
was most enjoyable, and everyone very kind to me.
We had a capital passage, and landed at Glasgow
all right. The old country was looking so beautiful, the bright green of the fields and trees so
refreshing after the brown, dried-up appearance
of the prairie. The scenery of the Rockies is
very grand certainly, and the vastness of America
very impressive; but for quiet beauty, and a

nse of rest, comfort, and home life, it ᴄₐₙₙₒₜ ᴄₒₘpare with **England**.

I have been home some months now, and enjoy it all very much; but, all the same, I long for my active, busy life out West. I have never been so well, and could not have been happier anywhere, than I was during my two years out there, and the best proof of this is that I am longing to be back again, and look forward to the day when I shall set foot on the great ocean steamship, and set my face once more towards my mountain home in the Rockies.

I. R.

London: Printed by W. H. Allen & Co., 13 Waterloo Place. S.W.

HEALTH PRIM

Cloth, One Shilling each.

EDITED BY

J. LANGDON DOUN, M.D., F.R.C.P.
J. MORTIMER GRANVILLE, M.D.
HENRY POWER, M.B., F.R.C.S.
JOHN TWEEDY, F.R.C.S.

.EMATURE DEATH : ITS PROMOTION & PREVENTIO`.

.COHOL : ITS USE AND ABUSE.

`ERCISE AND TRAINING.

E HOUSE AND ITS SURROUNDINGS.

*THS AND BATHING.

`ERSONAL APPEARANCE IN HEALTH AND DISEASE.

`r`E SKIN AND ITS TROUBLES.

`THE HEART AND ITS FUNCTIONS.

.THE NERVOUS SYSTEM.

HEALTH IN SCHOOLS.

LONDON :
W. H. ALLEN & CO., 13, WATERLOO PLACE, S.W.

ent Women Series.

Crown 8vo.   3s. 6d. each.

ALREADY ISSUED :—

GE ELIOT.   By MATHILDE BLIND.

GE SAND.   By BERTHA THOMAS.

IA EDGEWORTH.   By HELEN ZIMMERN.

LY BRONTË.   By A. MARY F. ROBINSON.

RY LAMB.   By ANNE GILCHRIST.

ARGARET FULLER.   By JULIA WARD HOWE.

LIZABETH FRY.   By MRS. E. R. PITMAN.

OUNTESS OF ALBANY.   By VERNON LEE.

HARRIET MARTINEAU.
                    By MRS. FENWICK MILLER.

MARY WOLLSTONECRAFT GODWIN.
    By ELIZABETH ROBINS PENNELL.

RACHEL.   By MRS. A. KENNARD.

MADAME ROLAND.   By MATHILDE BLIND.

SUSANNA WESLEY.   By ELIZA CLARKE.

MARGARET OF NAVARRE.
                    By A. MARY F. ROBINSON.

MRS. SIDDONS.   By MRS. A. KENNARD.

MADAME DE STAËL.   By BELLA DUFFY.

LONDON : W. H. ALLEN & Co., 13, WATERLOO PLACE.